Dominic sighed and let his head drop against the pillow.

He was desperate to stop Caroline from moving away. A quick jerk of her wrist and she'd be stretched out flat against his chest. Another twist and he'd have her on her back. A button undone and a lowered zipper and he'd be pushing inside her warmth.

With everything he'd learned about her in the last month he could woo her. Seduce her. Prove to her that their connection was special and could survive anything.

He could win back her love.

If not her trust.

Dear Reader,

This book was inspired by an advertisement I read in one of those fancy magazines you find on an airplane. You know the kind—they sell foot massagers and battery-operated wine openers. This particular ad was for an exclusive matchmaking service that I seriously considered using. When I called the number listed I was told that the initial fee was $10,000. I figured I would try to find Mr. Right for free first.

Well, my search is still on, but this story is for everyone who has had success on the Internet or through dating services. If you believe the commercials on television, it really can work. Just as it did for my hero and heroine, Dominic and Caroline…after a few bumps in the road, that is.

I love to hear from readers. Come visit me at my Web site, www.stephaniedoyle.net.

Happy reading!

Stephanie Doyle

STEPHANIE DOYLE

Suspect Lover

Silhouette®

Romantic

SUSPENSE

SILHOUETTE BOOKS

ISBN-13: 978-0-373-27624-0
ISBN-10:   0-373-27624-9

Recycling programs
for this product may
not exist in your area.

SUSPECT LOVER

Visit Silhouette Books at www.eHarlequin.com

Printed in U.S.A.

Books by Stephanie Doyle

Silhouette Romantic Suspense

Undiscovered Hero #792
Suspect Lover #1554

Silhouette Bombshell

Calculated Risk #36
The Contestant #52
Possessed #116

Silhouette Duets

Down-Home Diva #65
Bailey's Irish Dream #88

Silhouette Flipside

One True Love #2
Who Wants to Marry a Heartthrob? #23

STEPHANIE DOYLE

a dedicated romance reader, began writing her own romantic stories, some funny, some adventurous, but all delivering the quintessential happy ending, at age fifteen. At eighteen she submitted her first story to Harlequin Books and by twenty-six she was published. Now in her thirties, she struggles between the demands of her "day" job, her writing and trying to find a little romance of her own. She lives in South Jersey with her two cats, Alexandria Hamilton and Theodora Roosevelt. She wants to get a dog, but the cats have outvoted her.

To Eric and Brian.
Here's another book for you.
Love, the Book Lady

Chapter 1

"We're here, ma'am."

Caroline tore her gaze away from the structure on the hill. Realizing that the limo had stopped, she smiled politely at the driver in the rearview mirror.

"Different, isn't it?" he said pointing with his chin in the direction of the architectural nightmare that was her destination. The stone slab building jutted out from the cliff like a bad sandcastle that had been pounded by too many waves.

It could be her next home. Possibly. Maybe. Wow. It was ugly.

"I've never seen anything like it," she admitted.

The driver chuckled and shifted his weight to exit the car. A second later, her door was opened and a helpful hand waited for her.

"Can't say it's the boss's style, either," he noted. "He's more the downtown condo type if you know what I mean. But he likes his privacy."

Caroline imagined he must. She looked around and saw only the ocean to her right and to the left the stone structure precariously perched on the cliff.

"What am I doing here?" she mumbled to herself as she struggled against the very logical urge to get back in the car, return to the airport and fly home.

Dear Ms. Somerville,
I received your profile from the service we've both chosen to utilize. I believe we might be compatible.

I understand you are a writer. That sounds like a very interesting profession. What would you like to know about me?
Sincerely,
Dominic Santos

"Excuse me, ma'am did you say something?"

Caroline snapped back to attention to find the driver dripping in luggage. She offered to take one of the bags but he smiled and headed for the house. She followed him to what she supposed was the front door. Only it didn't look like any door she'd ever seen as the stone slab portal was skewed to the right. The driver rang the doorbell.

She wasn't ready to do this. She wasn't ready to meet this man right here, right now. Everything she'd hoped for, dreamed of and wanted was potentially beyond that door. Her breath caught in her chest. She might faint.

At his feet.

That would make a heck of a first impression.

The door opened and a young woman with short spiky hair wearing a top that didn't quite cover her stomach and a skirt that didn't quite cover her thighs greeted them both. "Hi! You must be Caroline. Mr. S. told me to let you in."

A large black dog muscled past the girl to greet the new guests. Caroline instantly offered her hand for the dog to sniff, which it did before licking it affectionately.

"Oh, sorry," the girl apologized. "Don't mind her. She doesn't bite or anything. Her name is…"

"Munch," Caroline finished. "Her name is Munch."

Dear Mr. Santos,

I received your profile. It was quite detailed. But I imagine that's part of the sizeable fee we're paying. This isn't like any other matchmaking service, is it? Annual gross income, detailed personality profiles, education history. One might think we were applying for a job with the CIA rather than just looking for someone. You asked what I wanted to know about you. So many things, I suppose. What you like. What you don't like. Your hobbies, your passions. Why you chose to go this route to find a wife.

As for me, you were right in saying I'm a writer, but I have to confess it's not as exciting as most people believe. I spend a lot of time on my own. I had a cat, but he recently passed away. I'm thinking of getting a kitten. They are great company.

Regards,
Caroline

"Come on in. Mr. S. said to show you around the place."

"He's not here?" Caroline tried to decide whether she was disappointed or relieved.

"Gosh no, Mr. S. is like never here. I take care of Munch during the day. I walk her a few times and sometimes I even have to come back in the evening if Mr. S. is pulling an all-

nighter. This is the foyer, obviously. Off to the right is the
kitchen. It's totally tricked out with the best appliances."

Caroline nodded and reached down to find Munch
pressed up against her leg. She rubbed the animal's short
silky fur and thought how sad it was that such an affectionate creature was so often left alone by her master.

"Down those steps to the left is the living room. There
is a really cool flat-screen over the fake fireplace. Then
from there down another few steps is the pool house. Wait
until you see that. It's wicked."

Tuning out her tour guide, Caroline tried to study her
surroundings. A house could say so much about the person.
Hers certainly did. Every stick of furniture she'd chosen.
Every picture she'd hung. Antique pieces mixed with
modern. The local artist she discovered at a small gallery
opening in D.C. There was her mother's milk pitcher col-
lection. Her aunt's dolls. Those she held on to, too. But they
were still part of her.

There weren't many pictures on Dominic's wall. Two
modern-art blasts of color that were probably recom-
mended by a decorator. The few items of furniture were
quality, but the space still seemed empty. The outside was
a study in cutting-edge architectural design with rounded
stone levels that resembled a weathered staircase. The
inside reflected none of that radical theme.

Caroline followed the girl, who had eventually introduced herself as Cindy, to another open area that on one
side looked like a very high-tech office space and on the
other an advanced gym. Her attention was quickly captured
by the pool that gleamed through the glass doors.

Drawn to it, she ignored Cindy's explanation of the
various different aerobic machines and opened the door
that led to what was a room entirely enclosed in glass. The

smell of chlorine punched her in the face, but it was a clean smell. Beyond the pool, looking out the glass walls she could see the waves rolling up against the sand below. The effect was amazing. She predicted that swimming in this pool would feel like swimming high on top of the ocean.

"I know," Cindy said apparently reading Caroline's thoughts. "Isn't it, like, so awesome? Mr. S. says I can swim in it any time I want when I'm here. And in the winter it's heated."

Caroline nodded. Yes, it was awesome.

Dear Caroline,

My hobbies, my likes, my passions all revolve around the same thing: my work. My partner, Denny, and I founded and built Encrypton into a successful business. We've recently taken on a new partner to help grow it into something even bigger. It's a very busy time for us. I want to be clear—I am what most would consider a workaholic. I don't apologize for that and I don't see it changing. You asked why I chose this method to look for a wife. The truth is, this was the least time-consuming. If you would still like to communicate perhaps I could call you.

Dominic

P.S. I have a dog. You mentioned you once had a cat. I don't know if you like dogs. Her name is Munch. She used to chew things as a puppy.

"That's the tour," Cindy proclaimed as they stood in what was Dominic's master bedroom. More glass walls provided another perfect view of the ocean. It was an odd contrast, this sense of isolation mixed with a feeling of openness.

"I appreciate you showing me around."

"No problem. I guess I'll go. You're okay with Munch, right?"

The dog was plastered against her thigh and her tail was wagging so hard Caroline wondered if the poor thing would shake apart. Maybe she knew that Caroline had come to give her company.

"I'm fine. Enjoy the rest of your day."

Caroline didn't bother showing the girl out. She didn't feel completely comfortable with the ritual as it wasn't really her place. She was more of a guest than Cindy.

When the house was completely quiet she sat on the bed and saw that her suitcase had been left in this room. His room.

"Can I tell you a secret, Munch?"

"Roof!" Munch replied.

"I'm really a coward."

"Roof. Roof."

"No it's true. I thought I wanted this. A husband. A baby. But now I'm not sure this is the right way. I don't even know this person. I don't know if I can do this. If I'm brave enough."

"Roof. Roof!"

"All right. If you say so."

Caroline patted her new friend's head and contemplated the large king-size bed behind her. She was so tired. From the trip, the anticipation, the anxiety. Lying down, she instantly felt a dip as Munch leaped onto the bed with her and settled down at her back. The faint hint of a masculine aroma drifted up from the pillow. Caroline thought it smelled rather nice.

She reached behind her and patted Munch. The dog's presence was ridiculously reassuring. "Seriously, what if this is the biggest mistake I've ever made in my life?" she whispered.

This time there was no answer.

* * *

Dominic Santos stared out the window of his office which overlooked a valley that, despite its name, wasn't really made out of silicon. Frustrated by how little he'd done all day, he returned to his desk but only to check the time on his computer again.

It was only one minute since the last time he looked.

What the hell was he doing? He was behaving like some love-struck teenager and he didn't appreciate the feeling. That's not what this visit was about. This was a test—for both of them—nothing more.

Four days to determine their compatibility and their adaptability. Four days to see if the service had correctly matched them based on their personalities and life goals. There was absolutely nothing to be nervous about. They had e-mailed and spoken on the phone for several weeks now. This was just the next step.

Abruptly he opened the drawer of his workstation and removed the manila folder inside. Flipping it open, he caught his breath as her picture smiled up at him. Beneath it were copies of their exchanged e-mails. He wasn't sure why he'd felt the need to print and save them, but he had. He lifted the photo and studied it. It hadn't changed since he'd first gotten it. It still captivated him.

Dear Dominic,

I enjoyed our conversation last night. I hope you don't mind the follow up e-mail. Words tend to fall easier from my fingertips than they do my mouth. I know I hesitated regarding your offer, but I have had a chance to think about it and I will accept. I would feel more comfortable paying for my ticket. I have some revisions to finish up on my latest manuscript, but, say in two weeks?

I suppose it's time we met.
Caroline

Dominic cursed, put away the folder and checked the time again. He wasn't pleased to see that it hadn't changed.

She had to be at the house by now. He had his secretary, Serena, call the airline to verify that the plane had landed on time. It had. Given that information, then factoring in the time it would take for her to freshen up, meet Henry at the baggage claim, get underway, and allowing for the traffic at this time of day, he calculated that she should be arriving at his home a little after five.

It was 5:01.

Perhaps he should leave now. It would take him a little more than an hour to get home in the rush hour. Plenty of time for her to get settled, maybe even take a nap to fight off the jet lag. Or maybe he should call first to see if she was there yet.

He picked up the phone and then put it down. Just like he had at least a dozen times this past week. Once she'd made the decision to come, he hadn't felt the need to continue calling her. No, that wasn't true. He'd wanted to talk to her; he just hadn't wanted to give her an opportunity to change her mind. He had, however, sent another e-mail.

Caroline,
I must insist on paying. You're making the trip. Let me at least do this. I've booked your ticket, first class. Attached is the itinerary.
Dominic

No, calling would have been overkill. If he'd missed the sound of her voice after talking nearly every day for a week, then it was a small price to pay for not jeopardizing this meeting. Dominic hoped his strategy paid off. After all he knew the plane had landed. He just didn't know if she'd been on it.

Impatiently, he hit his intercom. "Serena."

"Yes, Mr. Santos?"

"Get Henry on his cell phone, will you? And put him through to me."

"Yes, Mr. Santos."

Dominic turned back to his computer and tried to focus on work, but gave up when his eyes once again strayed toward the clock. This was insanity, and frankly it was pissing him off.

Maybe this was all a big mistake.

His intercom beeped. "That's Henry on line one, Mr. Santos."

Dominic snatched up the receiver. "Where are you?"

"Just leaving Half Moon Bay, sir. Ms. Somerville's plane arrived on time. I dropped her off at the house a few minutes ago. Was there anything else you needed today?"

"No. That will be all."

He hung up the phone and tried to convince himself that the overwhelming relief surging through him right now had more to do with his plans and less to do with Caroline. He'd started on this path with a very specific goal in mind. He wanted a wife. He wanted a child. He'd taken the most expedient path to obtain the first objective by hiring an exclusive matchmaking service. Caroline's had been the third profile he'd received and the only one he considered making contact with. At first he'd been wary of the idea of a long-distance situation. She lived in Virginia, on the other side of the country from San Jose, California.

It was the picture. She wasn't strikingly beautiful, but she was pretty. And there was serenity in her face that appealed to him. It made him imagine that she was someone people found easy to be with, easy to look at. He'd gone to her Web site to see the photo she used for the back covers of her books. In that shot she looked even prettier, but the soft smile wasn't there. Instead she looked very studious.

He preferred the other picture. His picture. Now, he wanted to see the real thing.

Dominic beeped Serena again. "I'm going to be leaving in about thirty minutes. No more calls get through."

"Leaving for the day, sir?"

He heard the incredulousness in his employee's voice. In the ten years she'd been working for him, he'd never left his office before eight.

"Yes."

"Denny wanted to meet with you."

Denny. Damn.

His partner and senior programmer had sequestered himself in his office for the past few weeks working on a project that he said was explosive. Of course he wouldn't give any indication about what the hell that meant. Worse, his behavior was starting to alarm their newest partner. But Dominic had assured Steven this was Denny's way. All or nothing. And the end result had always been worth it.

Apparently he was finally ready to reveal the big secret.

Not tonight. "Tell Denny I'll catch up with him. And no more interruptions for the rest of the day."

"Yes, sir."

Now all he had to do was concentrate on work for thirty minutes. He checked the clock.

It was 5:07.

Chapter 2

She was asleep on his bed with Munch pressed up against her back. That was how he found her. Their first introduction in person and she wasn't awake for it.

Her blond hair brushed over her cheek and he could see the steady in and out of her breathing. Just like her picture. Easy to look at. A sudden and surprising surge of lust flooded him.

It wasn't that he hadn't thought about what it would be like to make love to Caroline. He had. While he only had a photo and the sound of her voice to work from he'd allowed his imagination free rein. It had been a long sexual dry spell for him so his imagination didn't have to work that hard. The idea that this weekend might serve two purposes was suddenly very real to him.

He wanted her. Badly. And he hadn't even seen her eyes yet. He told himself there was a chance he was willing himself to want her because it would make things so much simpler if they did marry. While he didn't have any romantic illusions about what his marriage would be, he sure as hell expected to share a bed. But as he felt his sex stir and grow, he knew he wasn't forcing his body to do anything.

He wondered how she would respond if he went to her and began kissing her in her sleep, arousing her before she was even awake. His very own Sleeping Beauty. He imagined her eyes opening just as he pushed himself inside of her.

"Roof!"

Startled out of his fantasy, Dominic looked over at Munch and scowled.

"Shh. You'll wake her."

Too late. He could see her eyes flutter open. She stretched out languorously, and the sight of her twisting on top of his bed didn't help to cool his ardor. As if suddenly realizing that she was awake and wondering what had brought her to this point, she turned her head and saw him.

"Hi," she said softly.

"Hi."

He watched as she sat up and smoothed her hair, clearly embarrassed to have been caught napping. She shouldn't have been. She was compelling in her rumpled state.

"I wasn't sure if this was the right room. The driver left my bags here so I thought…"

"You picked the right room." Dominic swallowed hoping to ease the gruffness in his voice. "I want you to have this room. It has a beautiful view. I'll sleep in the guest room while you're here."

"Oh. Okay."

She stood and he took in her tailored jeans and light-weight sweater. The soft pink color made him think of the inside of a shell and he couldn't help but wonder if she would be as soft to touch. She stretched out her hand.

"I suppose we should start with the basics. I'm Caroline Somerville."

"I'm glad," he said taking her hand, which was small and delicate in his. "You came. I'm glad you came."

She nodded even as she continued to watch him, study him. He couldn't help but wonder if she liked what she saw as much as he did. Dominic wasn't a self-conscious man, nor was he lacking in confidence, but this woman standing in front of him in her white socks was twisting him in ways he hadn't imagined. This was supposed to have been a practical and efficient way of meeting and interviewing a potential spouse.

All he wanted to do was kiss her.

"Roof!"

They both smiled as Munch hopped off the bed and maneuvered her way in between their legs. Dominic gave her head a rub and was glad to see that Caroline wasn't afraid or bothered by the dog.

"I've already met Munch. I think we're getting along very well."

"Obviously. You've already been to bed together." Dominic surprised himself with his attempt at humor. Sexual humor, no less. Probably not his strong point.

Still Caroline laughed softly.

"You must be hungry. I have food for dinner. I thought it might be better for us to eat here rather than at a crowded restaurant. Give us a better chance to talk without interruption."

"Did you just say you were going to cook for me?" she asked eagerly.

"Cooking might be overstating it. I plan on grilling."

Together they headed for the kitchen. While Dominic put together a very basic meal of steak and baked potatoes, Caroline tossed a salad.

"If you'll open the wine, I think we're ready."

Caroline selected the lone bottle from the wine rack mounted on the wall. "This is amazing. I love this label."

"I know. I read it on your Web site. It was on your Favorites list."

"You visited my Web site?"

Dominic wondered if he should have admitted that. "Of course. I wanted to see some of the titles you've written."

He turned away from the grill on the range and watched her smile grow. It was a large smile, practically taking up her whole face.

"I don't suppose you actually bought any of them? Authors need our royalties."

"You seem to do rather well with that. I've seen your annual income, remember."

Her smile faltered.

"I did buy one," he said feeling the need to make amends although he wasn't sure why. "I haven't read it yet, though."

"You don't strike me as having much time to read for pleasure."

"I don't."

She nodded. As she poured the wine and Dominic laid out the food, Caroline pressed him for information regarding his business.

"I don't want to bore you," he insisted between bites.

"You have no choice," Caroline insisted. "Unlike you, I wasn't able to get much from your Web site. Just products and services and half of that I didn't understand."

"Encrypton provides encryption software. We're not one of the bigger names out there but we're growing. Thankfully there is a tremendous demand. Government regulations require that much of the data being transferred over the Internet be secured. We secure it."

"How?" she pressed.

"Generally speaking, the data goes into a box, the box is locked, then transmitted over the Internet. Someone on the other end has a key that opens the box. We make both the box and the key. Specifically I couldn't tell you how the code works. That's Denny's department. I mentioned him, didn't I?"

"He's your partner."

"One of them, yes. Steven is the other. Denny and I... got together about twelve years ago. He had the idea for the program and I had a talent for business. Steven joined the company later, but recently took on the role of partner. He is our financial man. We're bidding on a large government contract and he's making sure we're in a position to do the work if we get it."

"I see."

Dominic poured her another glass of wine and prayed he wasn't boring her to death. She didn't seem bored, though. She seemed interested. "Ironically, I've been traveling to your side of the country lately. You said you were close to D.C?"

"Relatively. I live in Leesburg, Virginia. How does one go about winning a large government contract?"

"The biggest concern is stability. The government has to believe we can deliver. Second is getting the job done within the budget. I've been lucky to have some inside help. A former...employee of mine works for the FBI. Having dealt with the government for years, she's been giving me advice on how to speak their language."

Caroline's lips twitched at the edges. "You stumbled over the word *employee*."

"Did I?"

"If she was a girlfriend, you don't have to hide your former lovers from me, Dominic."

Dominic frowned. "She's not a former lover. She's a former employee. I wouldn't lie about that, Caroline."

He watched her shift in her seat and he could practically feel her skepticism. Reaching across the table, he circled her wrist with his hand. "I wouldn't lie about that," he repeated. "I have no reason to. If there was a lover you needed to know about, I would tell you. I hope you would do the same. I want us both to go into this with our eyes wide open."

"This?"

"Marriage," he said firmly.

He felt her retreat and regretted his haste in bringing up what was essentially the reason for this little get-together. But it was too late now.

"Caroline, you must know marriage is my goal. I believe I've made that very clear from the beginning. The point of the service we hired is not casual dating."

"I know," she said quietly. "You just startled me by talking about it so quickly. I thought we would have more time. I want to get to know you, Dominic."

"You know me. You know about my work. You've seen my home. I don't know that there is much else to talk about."

That made her laugh, but there was no humor in the sound. "What about your family, your friends? Your whole life before you started your business?"

"I have no family." He shook his head and forced himself to take a deep breath. Slow down, he thought. "That sounds more melodramatic than it is. My father left my mother before I was born. My mother died years ago. She was Mexican. My father was American. Is that a problem?"

"Your heritage? No. Besides, it was on your profile. But that isn't enough. It isn't nearly enough for two people to read each other's résumés, have dinner and then decide on marriage."

Dominic sighed and leaned back in his chair. "I don't have time for a drawn out romantic courtship. Hell, even if I did, I doubt I would be very good at it. I want to marry you, Caroline. I knew after a few conversations that ultimately you would be suitable."

She flinched and Dominic cursed under his breath. He was making a hash of the entire evening. He should have said nothing, had more wine and taken her to bed. The morning would have been soon enough to discuss the future.

Dear Caroline,
I told you my world resolves around work. However, last night during our conversation you seemed determined to find some other hobby or interest. I suppose I enjoy swimming, as well. I like the feeling of floating above the surface. Pushing my body in exercise. I love the freedom.
D

Unable to sit, Caroline stood up and wandered out of the kitchen and through the living room. Once there she could look down to the office and gym and from there see the glittering reflection of light on the surface of the pool. Beyond the glass house, the ocean crashed against the surf, leaving nothing but puffs of white to assure her that she wasn't lost in space.

It had taken so much courage to come here, she thought. So much to beat down the coward inside her. To pull herself away from her quiet little house and her quiet little town. The strength of ten men to leave her quiet little life and take a chance on the unknown.

She hadn't needed the therapist she'd worked with after her parents' deaths to explain the obvious. Her life, the life she'd known until she was sixteen, had been suddenly and irrevocably altered. It had changed her from a free-spirited teenager into a coward. Someone who always played it safe, who didn't take chances for fear of getting hurt again.

This wasn't safe. This had taken courage. Just to get on the plane and come here.

Only Dominic was asking for more.

"I don't know that I can do this," she muttered. It was the coward speaking and she hated it.

"Why did you come, then?"

She turned and found him nearer than she would have expected. Unnerved by his closeness, she took the stairs down to the pool room.

Maybe it was the pool that brought her here. His description of swimming gave him character beyond his curt e-mails. His one-syllable answers during their phone calls. It made her believe there was more to him. More of what she wasn't sure. It was too intangible to name.

"I asked you a question." This time he left a few feet between them but he still had followed her.

"Why did you pick me?" she asked instead. "Of all the profiles what was it about mine?"

He looked away and she wasn't sure if he was searching for the truth or the answer she wanted to hear.

"I picked you because of your career," he finally said. "I thought you would be used to a quiet life. Being on your own for so long, I didn't think you would make unnecessary demands on my time. Time I don't have to give."

The truth. It was certainly brutal enough. She supposed she had to respect him for that.

"I'm sorry if that upsets you," he said.

The truth couldn't upset her. It helped to ground her in a reality that was quickly slipping away.

"Answer me. Why did you come?" he repeated.

He took a step closer, his eyes fixed on hers forcing her to meet his gaze.

Why had she come?

Why hadn't she stayed home? With her work and her small circle of friends. Her fuzzy slippers and flannel pajamas. Why hadn't she just gotten a damn kitten?

Because you were tired of being afraid. Because you decided you could want again. A family. A chance at having a family.

That seemed too personal to share with him. Because it meant so much more to her than a simple word. She struggled to find an answer that would appease him. "I wanted to find…"

"Love?" he interrupted. "Surely you're not so naive, Caroline. Love is an aberration. At best a fleeting emotion that dies quickly once routine sets in. Two people of the same mind, with similar goals and compatible personalities can form a bond. A marriage based on that can be infinitely stronger than two people in love."

She didn't agree. But she didn't see the need to contradict him, either. "I was going to say happiness."

"I don't know about happiness." Dominic took another step closer. This time he reached out and took her hand. "But I can give you what you want."

"What I want?"

"A child."

She jumped a bit and he must have seen her reaction because he stilled.

"Your profile said you wanted children. You told me you even considered having a child on your own."

"I did," she blurted out. "I did consider that." But the coward had won then, too, convinced her she couldn't do it alone.

"You want a family don't you?"

The word was like a punch to her gut. It struck at the very core of who she was and what she'd lost and she realized that there was no point in holding back. Not if he was going to be her husband.

"I have no family, either. My parents were killed in a car accident when I was sixteen. I lived with an older aunt but she passed away two years ago. I've been alone. Not lonely. But alone. I decided I wanted more."

He nodded and she thought that he understood. A man who had lost his mother would know what it meant to start again. To take a risk and try to create a new family when you had already suffered the pain of losing one.

"Let me give you that."

"I'm thirty-five," she whispered even as he was tugging her closer. "It might not be that easy."

A hand reached up and slipped around her neck. She felt the warmth and the weight of it in her hair tilting her neck ever so slightly to the side.

"We can try. We can keep trying." He bent his head then and his lips touched hers. The bolt of attraction she'd been struck with when she saw him for the first time tripled, then quadrupled as his lips played with hers. His mouth opened and took possession. His tongue thrust deep. It had been so long. It felt so sinfully good.

Dark hair, dark eyes and the body of man who liked to push himself in exercise were easy excuses for his appeal, but Caroline knew it was the other things that coerced her into wanting him. His small barely-there smile. How his hand stroked Munch's fur. The way he held her close to him without suffocating her.

His head lifted and she knew he was staring down at her, but she didn't want to open her eyes. She didn't want to see the man she'd just met for the first time tonight. The man she'd only exchanged e-mails and phone calls with. Instead she needed him to kiss her again so she could go back to feeling as if she was in the arms of someone she'd known most of her life.

"Tell me you want this, Caroline. Tell me and I'll take you upstairs."

She lifted her hand to his chest and felt his heart beat heavily through his shirt. It was time to say that it was happening too fast. Time to retreat and head to her own bedroom. The coward was ready to bolt. But the fighter, the one who pushed her out of the house and on the plane to come here, the one who was willing to take another chance on life, stood her ground.

"Tell me."

His urgency was palpable and it fueled her need.

Tell him. Tell him.

But words wouldn't form in her mouth. Since they typically fell easier from her fingers, she reached up and cupped his face and then lifted herself so that she could kiss him in return. Letting him know in the only way she was capable of that yes, she did want this.

She wanted him.

Chapter 3

Caroline let Dominic lead her back up the stairs without a protest. She didn't want to tug on his hand, fearing he might stop. A stern "stay!" kept Munch happily curled up on the couch in the living room. Then the next thing she knew, she was standing in the bedroom.

His room.

She reminded herself that this wasn't like her. A woman didn't stay single as long as she had without having some reservations when it came to men. Sex was an important thing and she took it seriously. Maybe too seriously. But all her internal defense mechanisms evaporated with his kiss.

She should have known it would be this way.

Hadn't she reacted the first time she saw his picture? As if her stomach had plummeted to her feet. His serious eyes and serious mouth. When his name popped up in her e-mail, she smiled. His voice on the phone made her shiver. She wanted him before she'd agreed to his invitation.

She told herself it was her active imagination. That it was just the hope of what he could give her that made him seem so attractive. But she knew there was nothing imaginary about it. She'd come here for him. Because something inside her said he was waiting for her. And he kissed her not like a man bent on seduction, but rather like a man already in the grip of need. As if he'd wanted her before he'd ever seen her, too.

"Caroline," he whispered. His mouth left hers, taking her breath with it. "I'm sorry. I should go slower."

"No." She didn't want to go slow. She didn't want to have time to think. She wanted to act. Reaching down she pulled her sweater over her head, letting her hair fall in a muss about her shoulders.

The simple bra wasn't enticing and it hadn't occurred to her to wear anything more daring, but she could feel Dominic's eyes on her. With a gentle push, he turned her around so that she faced away from him. He bent her head forward and brushed aside her hair, his mouth falling hot and wet on the nape of her neck. His hands cupped her breasts from behind and squeezed.

The sensation was stunning. After so long—so long she didn't want to even think about it—of not being held or touched or treated like a woman, this was sensory overload. His fingers pulled down the straps of her bra until the cups gave up their hold on her breasts and his hands were there instead. He pinched her hardening nipples while his mouth made a trail down her spine. One sharp tug and the bra was gone. Then his hands were on the front of her jeans while his lips traced soft kisses over her bare shoulder.

She watched him undo the button and zipper, saw him

sink his hands into her practical white panties. The sensation of watching and feeling his fingers touching her sent a bolt of heat through her belly. Then he bent to pull off the rest of her clothes. Was it her imagination or did he linger over the socks? His fingers pulled them off. First one, then the other. His hand settled on her calf and even that simple touch made her shudder.

She could hear the rustle of material behind her and knew that he was taking off his clothes. Instinct demanded that she turn and help him. That she entice him with small touches and kisses like he'd done as he undressed her, but instead she stood frozen staring at the bed. Soon he'd be inside her and it would probably change her life.

A hand gently grazed her ass as he stepped around her. He sat on the bed and moved to the center of it, stretching himself out. The moon, high on a clear night, provided more than enough illumination for her to see. He seemed bigger to her without his clothes. More substantial. His sex thrust up high and thick from a dark nest of hair between his legs. His thighs were slightly separated, urging her, it seemed, to step between them.

"Caroline." Dominic reached out his hand to her.

Crawling—there was no other word for it—onto the bed and up his body, she settled her bottom gingerly on his belly, her arms pinned on either side of his head. His hands came up to play with her breasts again, his finger and thumb tugging on her nipple until her neck arched, then her back.

"Do we have a condom?" Her words were muffled as one of his hands circled her body. A finger traced her spine, ran over her bottom, then up her stomach until he once again palmed her breast.

"You can trust me. I'm safe."

She shook her head, as if to say that wasn't what she

meant. But he was pulling her head down toward him, his tongue playing with her lips until it pushed deep into her mouth.

"This is your decision," he muttered. He teased the corner of her lips making her want more than ever the deep impact of his kiss.

"Mine," she conceded. Her choice. Her life. Her decision. Her future.

She found herself shifting backward, twisting her hips until she felt the broad head of his erection butting up against her curls. She could feel how wet she was, knew he could feel it, too, and wasn't sure if she should be embarrassed by how quickly he'd brought her to this state.

"You have to help me," she said even as she reached down to bring him closer. She forgot how thrilling it was to hold a man's sex in her hand. To feel it pulse. Soft skin over resolute hardness. It beckoned her to take more. His hand was on her hip, guiding her and she could feel him sinking into her one hard inch at a time. Her body resisted at first, but his insistence and her slickness were no match for any defense she might muster.

Joining. Mating. The words were weak in comparison to how it felt to take him inside.

Instinctively she moved on him as he thrust up slightly. His knuckle found its way between her legs, teasing that perfect spot that made her see light even though her eyes were closed.

"More," he muttered. "Take more."

Opening her eyes, she wasn't sure what he meant. It felt as if she were already speared on him. But his eyes were closed and his jaw was tight. The muscles in his neck were corded as if he were in pain. It wasn't what she wanted for him. Her hands rested on his smooth chest and she used them for leverage as she sat up and indeed felt him slide deeper. Then that persistent finger between her legs, so intent on pulling on her, stroking her, catapulted her into a climax before she knew she was that close.

When the last tug of her muscles had subsided, he rolled her onto her back with gentle persistence. His face above hers, his mouth only a breath away. In the dark, the harsh lines of his cheeks and chin should have been frightening, but they weren't.

"Tell me if this is too much," he muttered in her ear, as his body lowered completely over hers. She felt him push into her and knew that she'd barely taken half of his erection. For a moment she wanted to protest. Her nails dug into his shoulders as her body was stretched and filled beyond what she thought she could take. She felt him stop and instinctively knew what it cost him. Focusing on relaxing, she tilted her hips toward him, encouraging him.

"It's okay," she muttered. "It's okay."

"I don't want to hurt you," he growled.

She could feel him pulling back. In retaliation she wrapped her legs around his hips. The action sent him deeper and this time beyond the pain she knew a fulfillment she'd never dreamed was possible.

"You're not hurting me." At least not enough to make her give up the pleasure of it.

His head dipped and he took her lips even as his body began to move more urgently. Each penetration was so deep. Before she could think about how one thrust felt there was another and another. It was too much. Too much heat. Too much power. Too much intensity. But she wouldn't have stopped him for the world. It was like being in the center of a storm. There was danger. A sense of fear. But also the thrill of watching it happen, of feeling it explode around her. She embraced it, all of it and relished in her triumph over the coward because for now it was gone.

For the second time she came and wondered if she might faint from the incredible rush.

Hanging on to her senses, she felt his body surge. She heard his muttered growl against her neck and felt the wet hot seed from his body pumping inside her. Caroline didn't realize you could feel that. Didn't know it was possible.

Slowly he eased away from her, rolling onto his back. She could still feel him between her legs and imagined she would continue to do so for hours. There was something entirely erotic about that. She rubbed her legs together and felt the wetness there.

Harsh short breaths from both of them broke the silence until she couldn't not say something.

"I can't believe we didn't use anything," she panted.

He said nothing.

She didn't turn toward him, didn't feel that she could. The intimacy they had just shared was suddenly gone. He wasn't touching her. Wasn't stroking her. She felt tears well up in her eyes and willed them away. This had been good. Amazing. Maybe he was nervous about the step they had just taken. Maybe he was as afraid as she was.

"You said you wanted to be a father, but I didn't realize you wanted it that quickly."

The bed shifted as he adjusted his weight toward her, but he still didn't touch her.

"I said I wanted a child. I have a legacy to offer. Something I've built. I want to give that to my child. What kind of father I will be, I don't know. I want to be honest with you, Caroline."

"You have been so far. I think."

She turned her head and saw even through the darkness

the stark white of his eyes. His hand reached out and settled on her stomach. A slow warmth built there and radiated throughout her limbs.

Finally. A touch.

"I don't imagine that I would make a decent parent. Or husband, for that matter. My work, it is who I am, not just what I do. But I will provide for you. I will never let anyone hurt you or our baby. I will be as much a part of your lives as I can. That has to be enough." He seemed to catch himself. "Is that enough?"

Was it enough?

Caroline glanced down at the hand that rested protectively against an unlikely conception. She easily could get up now, dress and leave. He'd given her a snapshot of her future, their marriage. An absent husband and father. She had no real ties to him. There were other men that the service she'd hired could set her up with. Another man might be more open to having a real family rather than simply inviting a woman and a child to come live in his house. If she'd found the courage to do this once, maybe she could do it again.

But that man wouldn't be Dominic. That was the true trap. Not some wisp of an idea that their relationship might result in a child.

"What happens if you fall desperately in love with me?" She smiled as she cupped his very stern face in her hand. She felt a muscle twitch under her palm and soothed it.

"Marry me, Caroline. Please."

Talk about a leap of faith. She might as well have been standing outside on the cliffs. She could turn back and take the safe path home, something she'd been doing all of her life. Or she could jump. She waited for the fear to creep up on her. Was ready to do battle with it. But there was nothing. Nothing but a sense of certainty.

"All right."

He thought she might have fallen asleep but it was hard to tell. The sex and the overwhelming release of his orgasm should have been enough to put him in a coma for the next few days, let alone hours. Instead he was staring at the ceiling.

A soft purr emanated from the space beside him.

Yes, she was definitely out. Dominic envied her sleep and wondered why he couldn't follow. Surely, he'd gotten the better of the deal tonight. He wanted sex. He wanted a conclusion. He wanted a child.

He received one, was promised the other and had the hope of the last.

His eyes were wide open.

Was it because of the feelings she'd invoked? Taking her, he'd gone beyond desire or need. Yes, there was the symmetry of motion that made for good sex. It was easy to label it chemistry. He'd had good sex before. He knew what it felt like. This was good and different. Memorable, but also unnerving.

That was okay. They liked one another. Lusted after each other. That would help make their marriage stick.

He didn't think that was keeping him awake.

It could be he had some antiquated notion that good sex automatically equaled a baby and as ready as he said he was for that, he wasn't.

He only wished he could make himself believe that.

There was no point in lying to himself. He was wide awake, listening to his fiancée—*his fiancée*—breathe because he knew that despite his declarations he hadn't told her the whole truth.

He should have told her who he really was. What he really was.

He should have let her know before she agreed to marry him that he could be dangerous.

Now it was too late. She was his.

Chapter 4

"Surprise!"

Caroline jerked back as a tall, svelte woman came bolting out of what was now her house and wrapped her in a ridiculously strong embrace.

"Oh, my God! I can't believe it. You are Dominic's wife. Of course he didn't tell me. Didn't give me any time to plan. If he hadn't mentioned to Steven why he was actually going to Vegas this weekend, we might not have known about you until you showed up at the office Christmas party. So typical of Dominic."

It took some effort, but Caroline was finally able to push her off. The woman stood over her by at least four inches and only two of those were because of her slim heels. Behind the affectionate stranger, Caroline could see a throng of people waiting for them inside the living room.

Oh, my.

A hand on her back nudged her inside and Dominic followed, dropping their bags in the foyer.

"Can you guess what this is? It's a surprise wedding reception! Tell me I surprised you, Dominic. Tell me." She moved around Caroline and leaned in to peck his cheek.

"I'm surprised," he said.

Caroline sized up the brunette elegantly dressed in white slacks and a black silk sleeveless top. Money. She wore it well. It was in the cut of her clothes, in the silver designer watch that dangled from her wrist, and the two-carat stud earrings that sparkled in her lobes. She watched as the woman slid her hands up Dominic's cotton-covered chest in an effort to balance herself while she leaned in to kiss him.

Instantly Caroline didn't like her.

Then she shook her head. *Wow,* she thought. *Jealous this quickly.* They'd only been married two days.

The brunette turned back and offered a dazzling—and Caroline tried to believe sincere—smile. "You must be Caroline. I can't tell you how excited I am to meet you. I'm sorry. This must be a shock for you. But I couldn't resist. When Steven told me Dominic was getting married, I couldn't believe it. I had to do something, so I just threw this little party together at the last minute. This way you can meet all of Dominic's associates and friends. Although with Dominic, that's usually one and the same."

"And you are?"

"I'm Anne. Surely, he mentioned me. I know he's tight-lipped, but come on, Dominic." Anne turned to Dominic with a chastising pout. "Really, besides Denny and Steven, I'm practically your best friend. And you didn't mention me to your wife?"

Dominic stood awkwardly in the foyer. He glanced toward Caroline, but didn't quite meet her eyes. Before she could wonder about that, Anne linked her arm and pulled her forward. "Come along. I'll introduce you to everyone. And then you can tell me all about how Dominic swept you off your feet."

Caroline followed the woman's lead, recognizing that despite the fact that she wasn't in the mood for a party after their tumultuous trip, she did want to meet the people in Dominic's life.

Servers worked the party dressed in formal black-and-white attire offering trays of food and flutes of champagne. The house had been decorated with masses of white flowers—roses, daises, even tulips. Elegant and not over the top. A quartet played on the lower level of the house. Sixty or so guests seemed well fed and entertained. All things considered, it was a very nice party.

Anne pulled Caroline toward a small group gathered by the window. One of the men was tall, lean and handsome with a deep tan and a pretty face. To his right was an older gentleman that Anne introduced first.

"This is my father, Russell Long. Daddy, this is Dominic's wife." Anne disengaged herself from Caroline's arm and headed off to mingle.

"It's a pleasure, my dear." The older man had the build of someone much younger than his full head of white hair suggested. Hair highlighted by a healthy complexion earned from either the sun or a booth. It was hard to tell. His eyes were fixed on hers and Caroline had the strangest sensation of being evaluated.

"Nice to meet you," she mumbled.

"Steven Ford," the younger man with the California looks announced. "Husband of Dominic's best friend and son-in-law to Russell here. Sorry to spring this on you, but once Anne has an idea in her head she's hard to stop."

"No, that's fine. I'm happy to meet all of you."

"It must have been a whirlwind trip."

"Yes, it was."

That and the most emotionally wrenching experience of her life. The two weeks leading up to the ceremony had been chaos. Dominic had flown with her back to Virginia to help her pack up her clothes and her most precious possessions. Her life. She'd been uncertain, emotional and tense. If it hadn't been for his bulldozer approach to each task, she might have changed her mind a thousand different times.

Instead he laid drop sheets on her furniture and promised her that once she was settled they could arrange another trip back to pick out the pieces she wanted shipped to California. He hadn't suggested she sell the house. An idea which she would have rejected as she'd inherited it from her aunt. It was the only connection to her family she had left.

But wasn't that the goal? She needed to break the connection to her past and embrace her future.

With Dominic. Her husband.

In the midst of all that, she'd learned she wasn't pregnant. Not that she wanted it or expected it to happen so quickly, but inexplicably she felt disappointed.

"And so this is everyone he works with?"

"Most of us, yeah," Steven answered. "There's a bunch of programmers. Plus some account reps, salespeople and support staff. And Denny, of course. Denny, come over here and try to be sociable."

Caroline spotted the man Steven was waving over. He wasn't hard to miss. Separated from the rest of the room, he stood alone with a beer dangling between his fingers. His gaze lingered on something or someone behind Caroline, but before she could turn her head to see what it was, he moved and was walking toward them.

Different from the rest of the men who wore slacks and sport coats, he was dressed in jeans and a T-shirt that had seen better days. His sandy brown hair was unkempt and overlong, as was his five o'clock shadow. As he moved closer, she could see that his eyes were almost bright red. Caroline hoped with fatigue and not drugs. There was no polite way to say it. The man was a mess.

"Hey," he nodded. "I'm Denny."

She held out her hand. "Nice to meet you."

"Yeah."

She wanted to say that Dominic had told her so much about him, but the truth was she only knew that he was a programmer. An excellent one.

"So you've got to tell me how all this happened." Steven nudged her. "Dominic literally walks into my office on Friday, says he won't be working this weekend because he's off to Vegas to get hitched and leaves. Please tell me you guys haven't been dating for years and I've been that oblivious."

Caroline smiled and found herself instantly liking this man. He had an easy way about him that was in direct contrast to his wife's intensity. "No, we haven't been dating long." She wondered what else to say, wondered how much Dominic wanted to reveal or conceal about their relationship. It wasn't that she was embarrassed about using the agency, but the speed in which it all came about might raise a few eyebrows.

"I met her in Washington."

Dominic came up behind Caroline and handed her a glass of wine. She took it gratefully.

"Yes," she added. "A mutual friend set us up. And there was a connection at first sight."

"Oh, isn't that romantic!" Anne who had been circling,

joined the group and beamed at the two of them. "And this was when?"

"Two months ago," Caroline answered her, counting the time from when he first contacted her rather than when they actually met.

"And Dominic never said a word," Anne repeated still evidently shocked by the news.

"He's entitled to a private life," Russell told his daughter.

"Yes, but surely you would tell your partners about your marriage," Anne said directly to Dominic. "In some ways it affects all of us."

"How so?" Caroline asked.

"Come on, Anne, nobody wants to talk about that stuff now," Steven said casually taking hold of her elbow and giving it a slight squeeze.

Anne huffed and then turned to Denny. Instantly she sighed and rolled her eyes. "You couldn't have at least shaved for the occasion? Really, Denny, sometimes you can be almost disgusting in your appearance."

"Sorry." He tipped the beer to his lips in a sort of toast. "Congratulations anyway."

"Thank you. But tell me more about you," Caroline urged him. "Dominic said you were working nonstop on some important new program for them."

There was silence and Caroline got the impression that tense glances were being traded.

"Yes, Denny," Steven said. "Please tell us what you're working on. I've been trying to get budget figures and projections on this latest endeavor for two weeks and I can't because you won't tell us what you're doing. You stay locked up in that cell of yours. You won't even come out for air."

"I don't want to talk about it." He shuffled his feet and took another sip of beer.

"You're supposed to be making sure our product is perfect before we make our presentation at the committee hearing next month," Steven scolded. "That better be done."

"The program is foolproof," he snapped. "I was working on something else. It doesn't matter. I'm done with it."

"What? You said what you were working on was important."

Caroline looked at Dominic. She'd never heard that angry tone in his voice before. His face was sterner than she'd seen in the last two weeks.

"It doesn't matter," Denny repeated.

"Boring. No one wants to hear about work, now. This is supposed to be a party," Anne said gaily.

Time for a change in topic, Caroline agreed. "When did the three of you become partners?"

"Actually, it was Denny and Dominic for a long time before I came on the scene and bought in," Steven explained.

"You mean until *I* bought in," Russell slapped his son-in-law on the back in a good-natured gesture.

"Right," Steven said tightly. "As for how Denny and Dominic met...you won't believe this but I don't think I even know that story. You guys started Encrypton twelve years ago, but how did you originally get together?"

"Forget that, Steven," Anne interrupted him, patting his arm. "No one cares how Denny and Dominic met. This party is about getting to know Caroline. I understand you're a writer."

The party continued and Caroline made the rounds and chatted to each of Dominic's employees. Deciding she needed a break and probably a bit of freshening up, she made her way upstairs. A few people lingered on the second floor loft, but not many. She smiled at them and made her way to the guest bedroom to check in on Munch, who had been quarantined.

Munch immediately left her warm spot on the bed to greet her mistress. She stroked the animal's head until the dog decided she'd had enough and returned to the bed to continue her nap. Caroline shut the door behind her and headed for Dominic's room. Her room, she mentally corrected. Her home, her bedroom, hers. It was going to take some getting used to.

She opened the door, but stopped when she saw Anne with another woman by the window.

"Caroline! Oh, good. I don't think you've met Serena."

The woman turned and smiled graciously. She was older, perhaps late forties, with dark hair pulled back into a severe bun. She looked tidy, if a bit conservative, in a navy blue suit.

"I'm Mr. Santos's assistant. I've been with him for a number of years."

Caroline shook Serena's hand. It was a loose grip, and Caroline noted that the polite smile didn't quite reach the woman's eyes. She didn't think it was personal, more like Serena wasn't the type to smile easily. She imagined that she and Dominic worked well together.

"We were just up here swapping recipes. Serena makes a burrito with homemade salsa that is simply to die for."

"You'll have to share."

The older woman's head dropped once formally. "I'll send the recipe home with Mr. Santos tomorrow."

"I hope you don't mind us sneaking away up here. But this view…" Anne turned back to the window and sighed.

"Of course not. The view is incredible. When I first saw this house, I wasn't thrilled with the design, but living in it I can see what the architect was trying to accomplish."

"Openness," Anne answered.

Caroline smiled. She didn't want to correct her but there was more to it than that. Any big house with large rooms provided a sense of space. This house was about freedom.

"We'll get out of your way," Serena told her.

"I did want to freshen up a little. I must be a mess."

"Oh, no. Not at all," Anne crooned. "Maybe just your lipstick. You look a little pale. We'll leave you to it."

Yeah, Caroline thought. She and Anne weren't going to be buddies.

It was shame, too. For the most part, Caroline was a loner, but that didn't mean she didn't want to make friends in her new life. And there was the fact that Steven and Dominic seemed genuinely close. She'd watched them for a while during the party. Dominic asking Steven work-related questions and Steven firing back with sports news. Eventually Dominic had relented and Caroline learned her husband had an interest in baseball. Pals as well as partners. She doubted Dominic had many friends and she wasn't going to let Anne get in the way of that, despite her feelings.

She was tired, that was all. She would have Anne and Steven over for dinner and give it another try. Sometimes first impressions could be misleading. She made her way to the bathroom and checked herself in the mirror. Deliberately, she added a little blush but left her lips untouched.

Hours later after everyone had left, Dominic opted for a hot shower to unwind. When he came out of the bathroom to find his bed empty he was surprised.

It was late. After midnight. In the past few weeks, he'd learned that his wife liked to go to bed early.

He considered it his first compromise. He preferred to work to one or two in the morning, but if he wanted to make

love to her he was going to have do that first, sleep for a
while, then work.

And he definitely wanted to make love to his wife.

.   Just thinking about her made him hard despite having
had her that morning. And three times the night before. He
might have been worried that he'd driven her out of his bed
with his sex drive if it hadn't been for the way she wel-
comed him each time.

In his life he'd never known such pleasure. Or escape.

But tonight he was going to play it differently. He
planned to kiss her on the cheek and roll over like a good
husband. She was obviously tired from the stress of the
past two weeks. Anne's party certainly hadn't helped
things. He was going to shelve his desire and show her his
unselfish side.

Only his wife wasn't there to receive his noble gesture.
And where was Munch? That was the trick. The two had
become inseparable. Find the dog and he'd find his wife.

And he did.

Munch stood on the side of the pool while Caroline
drifted up and down in a lazy sort of backstroke.

"Hi. I was too wound up to sleep so I thought I'd have
a swim."

She wore a simple black suit, but seeing the way it clung
to her breasts made the muscle in Dominic's cheek twitch.
His wife had fabulous breasts.

"I'll leave you alone." There. That had been noble.

"Why don't you come in?"

He wondered if he hadn't mistaken the blatant invitation. "You're exhausted."

"I just said I couldn't sleep. I need to relax." She
drifted over to the side of the pool directly below him.
Her hand reached out and caressed his calf, and the loose

shorts he'd put on to search the house for her no longer concealed his erection.

He stepped back and pushed the shorts off, then dove over her in a perfect arc. By the time he came up for air, she had removed her suit and tossed it on the side of the pool. Munch gave a warning bark as the wet suit hit a little too close for comfort and she trotted off.

In seconds he had her pinned against the side of the pool. In his arms she felt silky and wet. In another second he was pushing inside her. Here she was silky, wet and hot. He was discovering that he needed this connection like he needed air. The idea scared the crap out of him, but for now he ignored it so he could concentrate on how good it felt. He lowered his forehead to hers and sighed. Her legs locked around his hips and he had to forcibly stop himself from thrusting or it would be over too fast.

"I'm sorry," he whispered. "I should have…" He was at a loss.

"Don't be sorry," she said and placed her lips on the side his neck. "Not about this."

"What is this?" He wondered if she would even understand what he was asking.

Then she grasped his face in her hands and met his gaze. Her eyes were so beautiful. So filled with gentleness. She smiled and he felt a tightness in his chest that he hadn't felt since long before his mother died.

Startled by it, he began moving inside her, letting his body take over, working out whatever he was feeling with a good hard screw. He pressed his hips high and hard against that sweet spot between her legs, hoping she was with him because he knew he was going to come and he didn't want to try and stop it. He heard a gasp and felt her tighten around his shaft. Without another thought he let himself go, his body a mass of sensation.

When he came back into his head, her arms were wrapped around his neck and she hummed a little in his ear.

"This was nice."

"Hmm." He thought about how much energy it was going to take to get them out of the pool. He had the irrational thought of letting Munch pull them out with a towel.

"So," she said softly. "Tell me about you and Anne."

His hold tightened around her body. He hadn't seen that coming. He should have.

His wife was no dummy.

Chapter 5

Dominic stared at the ceiling. After three weeks of marriage, he knew where every faint crack in the plaster was. Every heavy stroke of paint. Even in the darkness with only moonlight filtering through the glass, he could still make out the tiny little imperfections.

She was sleeping on his arm. Her mouth slightly open so that he could feel the warm breaths of air on his shoulder.

It was driving him insane.

He glanced down at her and realized he'd studied her as equally intensely as he had the ceiling these past few weeks. He knew about the dark freckle behind her right ear. He saw the faint wrinkle that ran across her forehead barely visible when she was at rest.

So serene. So at ease with him. So trusting.

Or maybe not so trusting.

He considered the question she'd asked about Anne three weeks ago.

He'd avoided answering by kissing her. He'd kissed her long enough and slow enough until they were burning up. He'd managed to get her out of the pool and back up to his room—their room—where he'd made love to her again. Exhausted, she'd fallen asleep before he had a chance to separate their bodies.

There had been no more questions about Anne.

He wasn't even sure what he would have said had she pressed the issue. There had been an incident. A year ago at a Halloween party Anne had thrown. He'd told her he didn't involve himself with married women and that had been the end of it. As far as he knew Steven never found out. And it seemed at least to him that whatever problems they might have had were behind them.

Anne and Steven were happy.

Dominic shifted in the bed. He wouldn't have thought he had any idea what a happy marriage looked like. But he imagined that he and Caroline looked happy. Why shouldn't they? He felt happy when he was with her, and the feeling was so foreign to him it was almost unnatural.

In the near month she'd been his wife, there were moments that caught him off guard. Times when he couldn't remember what life had been like before her or couldn't imagine how he'd cope without her.

It was too much. Too soon.

He found himself leaving the office early to be with her. Last week he'd walked through the door after a rough day at work and made love to her on the kitchen table. It was as if he couldn't stop himself. Not when she smiled at him with that damnable serenity etched in her face. The weekend before, he'd taken her to Carmel to show her his favorite view of the ocean instead of working from home as he'd done every weekend since he'd started Encrypton.

He was losing control and he didn't like it. This wasn't what he wanted. He didn't want to enjoy the warmth of her breath on his shoulder. He didn't want to crave sex with her all the time. He didn't want to feel the way she made him feel when she smiled at him.

It needed to end. Space. That's what he needed.

"Get off me," he said, his eyes still focused on the ceiling. He jerked his arm and twisted his body and felt her jolt awake. "Get. Off. Me."

"Dominic? What?" The sheets slid down her body as she sat up.

He pulled away to the other side of the bed. "You're suffocating me. I can't stand the clinging every single night."

He didn't look at her. Wouldn't look at her to see what his words had done. There was stillness from her side of the bed. That was answer enough.

"I didn't know," she said softly. "I'll go." She climbed out of bed and took a pillow with her.

He didn't stop her. Didn't go after her. The relief he felt when she closed the door behind her was almost pleasurable. Until the regret over hurting her descended on him and the loss of her made him ache.

He couldn't think about that now. Tomorrow he would apologize. And tomorrow he would come up with a strategy to keep her at arm's length. There was no reason to push her completely away. He just needed some distance.

Shifting back into the center of the bed that now seemed cold to him, he went back to staring at the ceiling.

The next morning, Dominic sat down behind his desk and waited for his world to realign. This is where everything made sense. This world he could control. But as soon as he reached for one of the folders in his in-box, he found his head spinning back to Caroline and what had happened last night.

The guest room door had been closed when he emerged from his bedroom shortly after 6:00 a.m. He hadn't slept a minute; he hoped she had.

Staring blankly at his computer he wondered how in hell he was going to fix what he'd done. But the screen in front of him offered no answers.

She was supposed to have been convenient. A sexual outlet, a sensible partner and a mother for a child he wanted.

Instead she was making him think things and feel things. Thoughts and hopes he'd closed off for so long it physically hurt him to consider making himself vulnerable again.

It was all about control. He simply needed to conquer his reactions and to a certain extent control Caroline. No more leaving work early. No more letting her talk him into a walk on the beach or a late-night swim. No more making love to her outside of their bed. In bed it was about marriage. About making a baby. That's all he'd let it be.

There. It was a plan.

Forcing himself to concentrate on work, he picked a folder from the top of the pile. Immediately he saw that it wasn't the one he'd left there on Friday. He might have thought he remembered incorrectly if he didn't know himself that well.

He hit the intercom buzzer. "Serena, can you come in here."

"Yes, Mr. Santos."

A second later the door opened.

"Was someone in my office on Friday after I left?"

She hesitated for a second. "Yes, sir. Steven came by looking for you. You left a little early, remember?"

Caroline's fault. She'd wanted to go out to dinner. He'd relented. No more.

"He said he needed some figures for the budget he's preparing. He said he just needed to check a folder. I let him in."

"That's fine. Thank you."

"He's scheduled to meet with you this morning."

"I know. Let him in as soon as he gets here."

She nodded and left. Dominic reorganized the folders the way he wanted them. He was being anal. He didn't pretend otherwise, but order was as necessary to him as food. As important as making love to Caroline was becoming.

Don't think about her.

"Hey there," Steven greeted him with a wave as he entered the office and shut the door behind him.

"You were in my office and moved some folders."

Steven stopped, startled by Dominic's response. "I needed the figures on the print ads we're thinking of running in some of the industry magazines next month."

Dominic nodded. "You should have called me."

"Uh, hello? Newlywed. You were off for a romantic dinner. I think you were actually smiling about it." Steven laughed. "Not exactly the kind of thing you needed to be bothered by."

"Nothing about my work bothers me and that isn't going to change because I have a wife." He wouldn't let it.

"Got it." Steven shrugged. He took the seat in front of his desk. "I wanted to talk about Denny. Do you know what project he was talking about at your party? He's been locked away for over two months in his office on what he said was software enhancement. Then it turned into something else. He told you it was the biggest project of his life. Now all of the sudden it's not important. I'm trying to get answers but he's gone hermit again and won't reply to any of my e-mails."

Dominic remembered the conversation but hadn't given

it that much thought. Denny was always working on something big. It was possible that he'd overestimated how important it was. Or maybe he couldn't get it to work. Still, it was unlike him to drop something unfinished.

"I'll talk with him today about it."

"Thank you. I swear I can't communicate with him. All he cares about are his programs. You try to have a conversation about anything else and forget it. He's such a geek. It's like he can't even look me in the eye when he talks."

"He's been through a lot."

"Like what?" Steven asked. "I'm in business bed with this guy—you, too, for that matter, and it didn't dawn on me until your wedding reception how much I really don't know about either of you."

"You know we're good at what we do," Dominic said softly. "What else do you need?"

Steven stood and ran a hand through his blond hair. "Look, I'm sorry. It's just Russell is on my ass to make sure this company gets that government contract and makes good on *his* investment. Sometimes I think I never should have taken his money, but I know this business is about to explode. Did you see the article in the *New York Times*? Someone cracked the encryption code on data being sent to a major insurance company in Los Angeles. It's the second incident this month. That kind of bad publicity for our competitors is gold for us. Especially now."

"I know."

"So I can trust Denny. When he says the code is foolproof, it's foolproof, right?"

"You can trust me. I wouldn't let Denny put out a product I didn't know he believed in. As for his special project, if I think it's worth his attention I'll convince him to pursue it again."

Steven nodded. "Okay." He turned to leave but stopped. "So it's been three weeks. How is married life treating you?"

Wonderfully. Horribly. How the hell was he supposed to answer that? "Fine."

"It's got its perks. But it can also be a kick in the pants."

"I'm discovering that," Dominic said.

"Anne wants to have you two over for dinner. Do something a little more intimate than the party she sprung on you."

"That sounds okay."

"Not that it will matter." Steven shrugged with a smile. "I doubt they're destined to be BFFs."

Dominic's gut clenched. "What makes you say that?"

"It's obvious. Anne is Anne. She's like a force of nature. Caroline seems more like the reserved type. Quiet."

An irrational anger zipped through Dominic at the mere thought of comparing the two women. It startled him so much he deliberately didn't defend her. "Caroline is quiet. Yes. But like you said we're partners in this business. In bed together figuratively. That means our wives are too, to some extent."

Steven nodded. "I imagine you two are probably going to want to start a family right away."

The personal nature of the request surprised Dominic but he couldn't say it was out of character. The longer he knew Steven, the more he realized he was coming to count on the man as a friend as well as partner. Now having something in common other than the business, Steven had been making an effort to take that relationship further.

Or he could have another reason entirely for asking him the question. Either way, Dominic figured he deserved the truth.

"Yes."

He smiled a little sadly. "Anne wants to wait a bit longer. Says she's not ready to be anyone's mommy yet."

Dominic didn't know what to say in response. But when Steven didn't leave he tried to sound encouraging. "Soon. I'm sure."

"Thanks. You'll let me know what happens with you and Denny."

"I will."

Caroline watched the clock on her desk. The short hand pointed to the seven and the long hand tipped past the twelve. Long since done working, she turned off her laptop and tried not to think about how little she had accomplished.

She hadn't eaten much all day and, given the time, knew she should be famished, but she wasn't. Her stomach was too filled with dread. He'd be home eventually. He would walk through the door like he'd done since she'd been living in his house—her home—and what?

Would he lean down and kiss her as he'd gotten into the habit of doing? Would he apologize for being an ass and fall at her feet begging for forgiveness? Would he say that he'd lied and she didn't really suffocate him?

Or would he simply behave as if nothing had happened. As if he meant it.

That would be the real lie. She'd been sleeping in the same bed with him for over a month. If she moved away at all during the night, he would either follow her or pull her back against his side. He'd never felt *suffocated* before.

Five weeks, she thought desperately. Five weeks of knowing him, three weeks of being married to him and already she was crazy. Angry and hurt.

Afraid.

Slamming her hands down on the desk, Caroline stood. Unapologetic that she'd startled Munch.

This wasn't how it was supposed to be. She didn't want

all this. Less isolation. Less fear. Maybe a family. That's all she wanted. All she imagined she could have when she'd decided to be something else besides a coward.

Instead he invaded her thoughts throughout the day. He was in her dreams at night. When he touched her, she felt things that she never thought were possible. Making love to him had taken on an importance she'd never believed possible.

And with a few short sentences, he'd wreaked havoc.

Now the fear was back and it made her want to leave him. To go home now before he could hurt her any more.

But she wouldn't go. She knew she needed to hang on. To fight. For him as much as for her.

The front door opened and Munch leapt up to welcome her master home. Caroline watched as he patted the dog's head and dropped his briefcase in the foyer. He looked around and saw her. She'd set up her office in the living room.

"Hello."

She lifted her hand negligently. "Hey."

"You've been working."

Not really. "Yes. New project. I like to outline first."

"Have you eaten?"

This was awful. Her heart shouted at her. *Say something. Do something. You are married to this man. Fight for him!*

But Caroline just shook her head. "There's some left-over pasta from last night. I can heat it up."

"I'm just going to change."

Change, she thought. How about from the cold distant man who was standing in the foyer back into the one who last week had come home after a day of work and lifted her onto the kitchen table and made love to her until she'd screamed with ecstasy?

It might have been minutes or an hour before she heard

his footsteps coming down the stairs. Only then did she realize she hadn't moved from her spot near her desk. Quickly she made her way to the kitchen and stuck her head deep inside the refrigerator so she wouldn't have to look at him.

The cold began to numb her nose until she was forced to extract the pasta. She jumped when she saw how close he was standing. She opened her mouth to say something curt, maybe even something spiteful, but the words wouldn't come.

"I'm sorry."

Slowly she released the breath she'd been holding.

"I didn't mean what I said last night. I was irritated about something else and I took it out on you."

"Irritated about what?"

"It doesn't matter."

"I think it does. I'm not an expert but I'm pretty sure we're supposed to talk about what bothers us."

His lips thinned and she could see that there was something else bugging him. He didn't want to have this conversation with her now. He just wanted the argument to be over. This was good, she decided. She was learning him.

"Something happened at work today?"

His jaw twitched and he looked away from her. She watched him shake his head slightly as if debating what he would tell her.

"You don't have to tell me."

"No, it's not that. I don't know if I should. I need to think it through. Denny did something. I'm not even sure how to describe it. Maybe dangerous."

"Dangerous?" She thought back to the awkward man she'd met at Anne's surprise reception. Dangerous certainly wasn't a word she would have attributed to him. Nervous, though. He'd definitely been nervous.

"Let's forget it. I wanted to apologize. I've done that. I don't want to talk about Denny. Not until I can get my head wrapped around it. Can we eat?"

Dismissed. As efficiently as he'd tossed her from his bed last night. For one second she thought to press him, instead she bit her tongue. This was a process. Learning him. Learning how to live with him. Learning how to fight, too. Like a book she could only deal with one chapter at a time. This wasn't over, though. Not by a long shot.

"Dinner was good," Dominic muttered. She felt a hand reach out to stroke her hair.

He was kidding. He had to be. His hand moved to her shoulder. The invitation was clear but she couldn't imagine he was making it. Not this soon after last night. His finger ran along her arm gently caressing her skin. She trembled at the contact, but pulled out of his reach.

He sighed. "I take it I'm not forgiven."

She heard the frustration in his voice and it triggered her anger. She told herself that it was a risk confronting him now. But apparently she wasn't as patient as she thought she was.

Rolling off the bed, her feet hit the carpet. "I'm not good at this, Dominic. I'm not a confrontational person. I'm an observer. A witness. A writer." A coward, she reminded herself.

But not tonight. Tonight she had to be brave.

Dominic threw off the covers and stood on the other side of the bed. Naked. Unashamed. Glorious. And pissed. "What are you talking about?"

"I'm talking about this tug-of-war we seem to be engaged in. You think I don't know what you're doing? I get too close and you push me away."

"I married you. You live in my house, sleep in my bed. How much closer do you need to be?"

"You kicked me out of your bed last night. I want to know why."

"I told you."

"You lied." She saw him flinch, but she pressed on. "There wasn't anything bothering you last night. You made love to me like you couldn't get inside me deep enough and then it was over and you were gone. Still beside me but gone. Last night wasn't the first time, either. You don't like to touch me after we make love or hold me. Fine, I can deal with that. But did you know that as soon as you fall asleep you always pull me back in your arms? I'm not a yo-yo, Dominic. Are you scared of what's happening? It's okay. I'm scared, too."

His cheeks flushed but he remained immobile. "I'm not scared," he said tightly. "I told you up front how this relationship would work."

"You told me you were a workaholic. I can live with that. As long as when we're together you let us be together."

He closed his eyes and shook his head. "What do you want from me?"

She took a deep breath. Held it and then asked for what she knew she really wanted. "More."

"More," he repeated softly. "More? When I've already…" He caught himself and crossed his arms over his chest. "Fine. What's more? You want me to talk to you about work?"

"No. Not the superficial stuff, anyway. It's like a practiced speech every time you come home. The office was busy, plans are moving ahead on the government contract. Denny's behaving strangely. You never talk about the people there. These people who share the biggest part of your life with you. I've been down to your office. Talked with them myself just so I could get to know you better. Do you know that Serena has a brother and a niece still living in Mexico and she's working to get them a visa? Did you know that there are rumors about Denny having a crush on a real live woman?"

"I don't gossip. It's not what I consider professional."

"Oh, please. It's not about professionalism. It's about you and your damn control. Everything in its place. Don't let anyone get too close. I see it in the way you eat, dress and work. But not when you make love. You lose it then, don't you? That's why you push me away."

"I don't have to explain myself to you." His expression was closed. Neutral. As if he were debating with a stranger instead of fighting with his wife. It infuriated her.

"Yes, you do," she snapped. "I'm your wife. You have to explain things to me. Tell me why you walk through life with these self-imposed bars between you and everybody else in the world."

"You're imagining things."

"Trust me. I couldn't have a created a character as screwed up as you. Not unless there was a reason." She circled the bed to stand closer to him, but didn't touch him. Partly because she was afraid he would step back and it would break her heart if he did. "Is there a reason? Were you abused? Did your father hit you?"

"I had no father."

"Then tell me something. You never talk about your past. It's like you were born the CEO of Encrypton. Tell me about the boy. Tell me what happened to him to make the man. Was it your mother? Did she abandon you?"

"Leave her out of this," he said his voice chillingly cold. "My mother loved me. I loved her. That's all you need to know."

"Then who? Who broke your heart, who taught you not to trust? Another woman? Anne? Or maybe that former *employee* in D.C. that you were going to see. Was it her? Did she hurt you when she left?"

"You're being ridiculous."

Not so ridiculous. There was a reaction in his face just then and despite what he'd told her, she would bet her life whoever that woman was, she wasn't just an employee. Fear seeped inside her gut. "I won't spend my life with a man who is in love with someone else."

"For God's sake, I'm not in love with anyone!"

With that the fight left her. "I guess not." She sunk heavily on to the bed.

He paced in front of her and she could sense his agitation. "Is that what you thought? That we would play house, have sex and in a month we'd be in love. You're not stupid, Caroline. You should have known better."

The strap on her nightgown dipped off her shoulder, but she didn't fuss with it. "I guess I should have. I didn't. I'm falling in love with you."

The silence above her was deafening.

Then finally he said, "I don't know what to say to that."

"I don't need you to say you love me. But I think I need to know that someday you could."

More silence. "I have to go."

Caroline jerked her head up. "Go?" She hadn't figured on that. Hadn't guessed he might run.

He disappeared behind the partition that separated the bedroom from the master bath and closets and came back dressed in sweats, his feet halfway shoved into sneakers.

"I'm going to the office. I need to think." He walked past her to the door, stopped and turned. "I never considered that I would hurt you. When I decided to do this."

She smiled sadly. "Never thought that anyone would fall in love with you?"

"No."

"Well, that's a problem. Isn't it?"

He left and Caroline felt the air being sucked out of her with his departure. Maybe she'd been stupid to confront him. Maybe she should have given it more time before she pressed him.

But she wanted him. All of him. Unexpected, but there it was. And she *knew,* knew, that he felt something for her. He had to. He couldn't touch her like he did and not be unaffected. But he was fighting it.

The important thing to remember was that this was only a skirmish in the war. Looking at it strategically, he hadn't said he loved her. But he also hadn't said that he couldn't love her. Instead he had retreated.

A very un-Dominic-like thing to do she imagined. On some level she frightened him and that could only be possible if he was vulnerable. That was good.

Rolling back onto the bed she tugged the covers over her and willed herself to relax. Only a battle. Still a long way to go. When he came home they could talk again. This time without the yelling. Over time she would convince him that there were worse things than being loved by his wife.

And she would tell him that she wasn't leaving.

She sensed that he needed to hear that. It had to be the first thing she said to him the next time she saw him. Everything depended on it.

Chapter 6

"Are you looking at me funny?"

Lieutenant Mark Hernandez of the San Jose police force asked the uniformed officer standing next to him in Dominic Santos's fancy top-floor office.

Mark had been staring out the window overlooking the city, wondering why a guy who had all of this would have done what he'd done. His disgust at the waste must have shown on his lean angular face because he could have sworn that the officer was looking at him strangely.

"No, sir."

Mark leaned toward the man who was still more kid than cop. He checked his surroundings, then asked in a low tone, "You got a cigarette?"

"You quit, sir."

"That wasn't what I asked."

"No, sir."

"No, you don't have a cigarette?"

"Yes, sir."

"Okay, now you're messing with me."

"I'm really not, sir."

In dire need of a single puff of smoke, Mark walked out of the office and surveyed the lobby, hoping to find someone whom he hadn't expressly forbidden to give him a cigarette. Instead he spotted the secretary who was still sitting behind her desk, apparently waiting for her boss to come walking down the hall any minute.

"We're done questioning you. You're free to go."

She looked at him, her face expressionless. "I work here."

"Trust me when I tell you your boss won't notice your absence."

"Mr. Santos wouldn't do what you think he did."

A loyal employee. It wasn't such a bad quality. "Go home. Serena, wasn't it?"

She nodded.

"He's not coming in today."

Her face fell and it seemed as if his words had finally registered. She pulled her purse out of a drawer and headed for the elevators. The doors slid open and as Serena stepped into the elevator, another woman got off.

She looked first to her right, then to her left as if searching for the appropriate direction to take. Not an employee.

She spotted him and headed his way with purpose.

She was short with dark messy hair that made her look like a pixie who had recently rolled out of bed. When she stopped in front of him the top of her head barely met his chin even though she was wearing what looked to be three-inch-high black pumps.

"You got a cigarette?"

The question caught her off guard. Then she assessed him. "Just quit, huh?"

"Okay, now *you're* messing with me."

"Quit years ago. The patch helped."

He pushed up the sleeve of his already-rolled-up Oxford shirt. On his upper arm was what looked to be a large Band-Aid.

"Give it time."

"Right. Oh, by the way, I'm police Lieutenant Mark Hernandez. I'm investigating a homicide. And you are?"

The woman reached into the small purse that hung over her shoulder and pulled out a square wallet Mark recognized instantly as identification.

"Special Agent Eleanor Rodgers. FBI."

She flipped open the wallet for him to see.

He studied it and saw that it was legit. "Don't you guys always come in twos?"

"You've been watching too many movies. What's the situation?"

"The situation is that Denny Haskell, partner and senior programmer, is dead. Murdered. His car was urged off a cliff where it burst into flames. Dominic Santos, another partner and CEO, is missing. The wife hasn't seen him since the night before last. The only person we know he talked to was his vice-president, Steven Ford. He called Santos here at his office yesterday morning to tell him about Haskell. He hasn't been seen or heard from since. I've got an APB out on him but so far no luck."

"You think he did it?"

Mark shrugged his shoulders. "I sure would like to talk to him about it. What's the FBI's interest in this?"

"The company is about to be awarded a prominent government contract to supply encryption software for the electronic data transmission of medical claims."

"Huh?"

"Washington was going to give Santos tax dollars. A lot of them."

"Checking up on the investment, then," Hernandez decided.

"Denny Haskell was Encrypton's head programmer. The government needs to know what's going to happen next. I've been sent to monitor the investigation and report back to my superiors. I'm not here to interfere."

"Encrypton," Mark said. "Isn't that where the super-hero is from?"

"That's Krypton."

"Right. Right." Like he didn't know where the super-hero was from. But he figured with the FBI it was always best to play the part of the local yokel. The less credit she gave him, the more obvious she might be regarding her motives. Besides, he knew with the FBI that there was usually more to the story. "You found out about this pretty quick. That identification says D.C."

She hesitated for just a beat. "Haskell's death was picked up on the wire yesterday. I was told to come out here immediately and check it out. I wasn't aware that Mr. Santos was missing until just now."

"Why you? I mean, why not some S.A. from the L.A. or San Francisco office?"

"I have a particular talent."

He lifted his brow. "That sounds interesting."

She smirked and he sensed he gave away his lurid thoughts. But really, a pixie with a particular talent? There was no way he wasn't going there.

"But you don't smoke, so sadly you're no good to me.

Also, you've got something on your nose," he told her brushing the right side of his own nose.

She swiped at it, but the tiny red mark remained.

The elevator door dinged and this time a haggard-looking guy, tall, blond, typical California, got off. Hernandez had already spoken to him. The third partner.

"What you're thinking is ridiculous, Detective. Serena just told me that you actually suspect Dominic."

"Until I can talk to the man...yep."

Steven ran his hand through his hair and looked over Mark's shoulder to the open door. "What's he doing in there?" he said, indicating the officer standing in Dominic's office.

"Waiting."

"For what?"

The elevator dinged again and this time another cop got off and made his way toward Mark.

"You got it?"

"Yes, sir." The officer handed over a folded piece of paper.

"You got a cigarette?"

"You quit, sir."

"Everybody is a freakin' Goody Two-shoes."

"What's that?" Steven asked.

"A warrant to search."

"What do you hope to find? Denny's car was pushed off a cliff. I doubt you'll find a murder weapon here."

"Just a second," the pixie interrupted. "If Haskell's car went over a cliff, how can you be sure it's murder? Maybe it was a hit and run?"

Mark looked at her. His instincts, which he considered to be flawless, were screaming at him. *Warning. Warning.* But since there was nothing he could really do about it, he decided to play it out. "It wasn't. There was another car on the road. And the skid marks of the second vehicle lead us to believe it was deliberate."

"So tell me again what you're looking for," Steven said.

"I sure would like to get a look at Santos's computer. I imagine there's a lot of stuff on it."

Steven laughed harshly. "You think a warrant is going to help? You're not going to be able to get past his security."

"Surely somebody has to know his password."

"Serena does but only sometimes. If he needs her to access something for him when he's off-site. But he always changes it right after that."

Mark cursed. He'd just sent the woman home. He turned to the officer with the warrant. "You know anything about computers?"

"I know they turn off and on," he answered. "I'm going to check in with the station and see if we got anywhere with the prints we took."

"The only thing I know about computers is they break when I touch one," Mark said humorlessly.

"I can help."

Mark and Steven looked at the agent.

"My special talent, remember? I'm guessing this is Santos's office?" She strode through the door and sat at the desk. The PC was left on; just the monitor had been turned off. When she pressed a button on its side the log-in and password box came up on the screen.

"So what do you do now? Guess?" Mark asked suspiciously leaning over her to watch her work.

"Guessing isn't my talent," she informed him. She hit a series of keys until the password screen was replaced by a blue screen with text covering most of it. She continued to navigate the menus using function keys and typing in commands. Five minutes later, she was once again looking at the password box. This time, she hit the Escape key and suddenly she was in.

The screen background was solid blue with the icons neatly arranged down the right side.

"What do you want to look at?" she asked Mark.

"I can't believe you got through it," Steven muttered.

"A flaw in the operating system. We just discovered it recently." she told him. "You all need to think about moving away from standard password protection. Do you know where Haskell saved his programs? On the network?"

Steven shrugged. "Honestly, I don't know. I never paid much attention to his work. My job is the money."

"Hey," Mark stopped her. "I'm running this little show, remember. And I don't care so much about Haskell's programs as I do about what Santos was working on."

She rolled her eyes. "Obviously, the two have to be linked."

"There's nothing obvious about it," he sneered. "I want the last thing Santos might have been working on. Can you do that?"

"Sure." The pixie computer whiz FBI agent picked up the mouse and started to navigate through a series of windows as quickly as she breathed.

It was almost dizzying. Mark looked away from it and focused his attention on the last partner standing. "Why don't you tell me again what he said to you on the phone."

Steven groaned "We've been over this already."

"You're the one who thinks he couldn't have done it. One more time won't hurt anyone."

"The police called me. They said they found my home number listed first on Denny's cell phone. It was in the glove compartment and survived the fire."

"Do you know why?"

"He might have been planning to call me for some

reason. I don't know. It's weird. He never called when he wanted to talk to someone. E-mail was his only form of communication. At least with me. How long he'd had my number, who knows?"

"Okay, okay," Mark said calming the man down. He didn't want him on the defensive. Defensive people rarely gave detailed answers.

"Anyway they called me, told me what happened. They told me that the crime scene was suspicious. What the hell am I supposed to do with that? I called Dominic at home and Caroline answered. She said he'd gone into the office."

"What time was that, when you called her?"

"Early. I think the police called me just after four in the morning. This would have been about four-thirty."

"And is that normal? For Santos to be at the office at four-thirty in the morning?"

Steven sighed. "He's a workaholic so it's not totally out of the question but something she said led me to believe that he'd been at the office all night. Again, not completely off the wall. It wouldn't have been the first all-nighter he pulled."

"Then you called here," Mark prodded gently.

"Yes. I called his direct extension and he answered. He started to say something, but I told him about Denny and he stopped."

"What was he trying to say?"

"I don't know. I wasn't really listening. I was about to tell him that Denny was dead. It was hard enough to process that information let alone share it."

"How did he respond?"

"He hung up the phone. I tried to call him back but he wouldn't pick up. I figured he was in shock. I know I was. Hell, I still am. Why would anyone kill Denny?"

Mark assumed the question was rhetorical, but he asked him anyway. "Why do you think?"

"I have no idea. He was a misfit. A computer geek. He spent the largest portion his life staring into a monitor. His interactions with people were few and far between. I can't imagine he ever got close enough to anyone to make an enemy."

"Do you know what he was working on?"

"I told you, I didn't follow his work. Although he was busy with a project, something he said was huge, but then he told us he was dropping it. Nobody knew what it was. Dominic was going to talk to him about it."

"Two days ago, you said." Mark remembered what he'd told him previously. Mark remembered everything, it's what made him a good detective. "Two days ago, Dominic talked to Denny about the project he was working on. That night Denny is murdered. You tell your partner the next morning and he vanishes. You didn't wonder where he was yesterday?"

Steven paused. "I guess I figured he went home. To be with his wife. I didn't come into the office until later."

"I have what you're looking for," the agent announced.

Both Mark and Steven looked over her shoulder to the monitor.

"That last thing he did was open this." She clicked on an icon and a picture of a woman Mark knew to be Santos's wife filled the screen.

"Ahhh, isn't that sweet," Mark cooed sarcastically. In truth it revealed a lot. The man was obviously smitten with her. A smitten man might not want to run too far. "Please tell me you can find the second-to-last thing he did."

She clicked on another icon and opened the last file that had been worked on.

"That's the company's financial statements," Steven said recognizing the figures on the screen instantly. "We needed them for our presentation before the subcommittee. Something is wrong. Those numbers aren't right."

He pushed closer to the screen and took control of the mouse moving the page down. "What the hell…"

"What is it?" Mark squinted, but didn't see anything but a bunch of numbers. Big numbers.

"I need to sit there," Steven said to the agent.

She vacated the seat and Steven took her place. He clicked open a few more tabs and studied them.

"What is it?" Mark wanted to know.

Steven opened his mouth, then closed it.

"Too late," Mark said instantly recognizing that whatever Steven had found wasn't good news for his partner. "Don't make me haul you down to police headquarters for questioning."

"These numbers aren't correct. They're not what I gave him," Steven said, the shock evident in his voice. "There's two million dollars unaccounted for."

"You're telling me he stole two million dollars from his own company."

"I'm telling you two million dollars is unaccounted for. There's a listing on these financials for a consulting firm whose services we never used. And the cash total is off that amount from when I finished the statements. I would have to check our accounts at the bank to be sure, but I know these numbers like the back of my hand. And that total is wrong."

"Who else would have had access to the statements?" Agent Rodgers asked. Mark shot her a look. So much for not interfering. She pretended she didn't see him.

"No one. Me and him. This is insane," Steven insisted. "Dominic wouldn't do this."

"Which?" Mark wanted to know. "Steal or kill."

"Either."

For a moment there was silence. Then the officer who had brought Mark the warrant stepped back into the office. "Sir, a word?"

Mark left the two behind the desk. "We got some hits on the fingerprints we ran. Take a look at this." The younger man passed him a fax.

Mark let out a low whistle. "Get out. The geek was a con?"

"So was the partner."

"Santos?"

The officer shook his head. "Not his real name. The prints we lifted from this office match Dominic Butler, one-time resident of the California Correctional Institution in Tehachapi, the same pen Haskell called home."

"What was he in for?"

"Assault."

"How long ago?"

"Seventeen years."

"Shit, he was just a kid."

"Pretty much. He went in at twenty, came out eighteen months later. Kept every appointment with his parole officer the year following, then disappeared. Not a trace of him in the system after that. He must have gotten somebody to forge him a new birth certificate. Because not long after, Mr. Dominic Santos, without a criminal record, arrived on the scene. He got a social security card, a license, opened up a checking account and got a credit card. Anybody looking might have found it strange that his life seemed to begin the year he turned twenty-three."

"Yeah, but if he never screwed up…"

"Then nobody would have bothered to go looking," the officer finished.

"Dominic Butler. Con and corporate genius. Okay, thanks."

Mark turned back to the office to find Agent Rodgers standing by the door. Steven was still behind the desk looking at the numbers, apparently trying to find two million dollars.

"You hear all that?" asked Mark.

"I did."

"I'm kind of surprised the government wouldn't have done a background check on the guy they were about to give all my tax dollars to." He studied her face then, but she gave nothing away. A cool customer, this pixie was.

"The government is interested in the product, not the man."

"At least this wraps it up."

"How do you figure?"

"He's got a criminal record."

"For assault seventeen years ago," she pointed out. "That doesn't make him a killer. Just an angry kid."

"It makes him a convict. And convicts are bad dudes. They don't come out of the joint rehabilitated. They just come out pissed. Seventeen years is a long time to go before cracking, but they all crack eventually."

"What are you going to do now?"

"I still have to find him," Mark said. "We have a warrant to search the house, too. I think I'll talk to the wife again. She was freaked yesterday when I talked to her but she's had time to calm down. And if anybody knows where he is, it should be her, right? I mean, the guy was ogling her picture. Eventually he's going to contact her."

"Your case. I'm just along for the ride."

"I take it that means you're coming."

"You take it correct."

"And if I have a problem with that?"

"You can talk to my SAC back in Washington and explain why the San Jose police department is refusing to cooperate with a government request."

Mark laughed. "Yeah, I thought you were going to say something like that. You know you're short for an agent."

He watched her get pissed off and knew he'd done it just for the fun of it, which really wasn't like him when he was on a case.

"I was recruited for my special talent," she informed him coolly.

"Turn the computer off. I'm going to send a uniform up here to claim it as evidence," Mark told Steven, who continued to shake his head in disbelief. "All right, Agent Rodgers, let's go."

Chapter 7

Caroline watched the men move through the house while Munch sat protectively by her side. A buzzing noise filled her head. The same sound she'd heard since she got the phone call from Steven saying Denny was dead. She tried to shake it off and turned her attention to the woman who had accompanied the detective.

She looked oddly familiar.

"Do I know you?"

The woman turned in her direction. "No," she responded.

"This is Special Agent Rodgers from the FBI," the detective introduced her as he walked toward Caroline. "She's here as an observer only."

Caroline continued to stare at her.

"I've been to a few book signings," the agent admitted. Then she reached out her hand to Caroline. "I'm a big fan. You can call me Nora."

"Fan?" the detective asked.

"Ms. Somerville writes novels. Mystery novels."

"Mrs. Santos," Caroline corrected her. "I haven't had time to change it yet legally, but I'm taking my husband's name."

"That might be a problem." The detective sat in the chair across from her and Caroline sensed the news wasn't going to get any better than it had been lately. "Ms. Somerville, how well do you know your husband?"

Not well. Not well enough to know why he might have left. Why he might be running. Only well enough to know that he wouldn't have hurt Denny. "How do you mean?"

"Did you know that your husband has a criminal record? That he spent two years in prison?"

The blow was sharp and it ripped the air from her lungs. Prison. Dominic. She forced herself to breathe in small pants and prayed she wouldn't hyperventilate. This couldn't be happening, not to her. Not to them.

Prison. Dominic. Criminal.

It couldn't be possible. He would have told her something like that. A man didn't get married and not tell his wife that he'd spent time in prison. She felt betrayed. The same way she felt when her parents had the audacity to get themselves killed in a car accident.

Caroline turned her face away from the two, knowing they were searching for a reaction. She focused on the glass wall that looked out over the hillside.

The glass. The space. It all made a twisted sort of sense now.

I couldn't have created a character as screwed up as you. Not unless he had reason.

The words came back to her in a flash. Along with the venom she was feeling at the time. A reason. That's what she wanted. What she had demanded from him. Now she had one.

She tried to answer, but her throat closed on her violently. She swallowed and tried again. "No, I didn't know."

"It was seventeen years ago," the detective elaborated. "I take it he didn't tell you."

"No, he didn't." So long ago, it could have been a lifetime, but that it still affected him was obvious. It was here in this house. In the control he exerted over his life, his emotions.

Dominic. Why didn't you tell me? "What did he do?"

"Assault," he said quickly. "Did he ever get violent with you?"

She closed her eyes, offended by the question. He'd never been violent. Violent would have meant losing control. Dominic didn't lose control. "No."

"Never lost his temper?" he prodded.

Caroline stared at the man. "Dominic is the most self-disciplined man I know. I can't imagine him being out of control." No, that wasn't true. He'd been out of control when they made love. But that was desire, not abuse, and all he inflicted on her was pleasure.

"Well, it seems he beat this guy up pretty good."

She flinched at his words.

"With his fists, though. Not a weapon. Truth is, two years is really the maximum on that sort of thing with no prior convictions. He must not have had a very good lawyer."

Caroline needed time to adjust and think. She didn't want to answer any more questions or hear anything else about Dominic. She needed time to understand what all this meant. But somehow she sensed that the detective wasn't finished.

"Another thing. Santos isn't his real name. After he got out of prison, he created a new identity for himself. You should know that your marriage to him isn't legal."

Funny, of all the things that had happened in the last two

days that piece of information hurt her more than the rest combined. She straightened her back and forced herself to listen despite the blows that felt almost physical.

"I'm sorry to have to tell you this."

"I don't believe you," she replied. "What do you want?"

"I need you to know the truth. I need you to know the kind of man you're protecting, if you are protecting him. I need to find him, Caroline."

"I told you yesterday, I don't know where he is."

"Can you take a guess as to where you think he might go?"

"No." She shook her head. "The office or this house. That's it. That was his world as far as I knew."

Nora leaned forward a bit, causing Caroline to shift her gaze to her. "How long have you known Dominic?"

"Not long," Caroline admitted reluctantly.

The detective pounced. "But you married him."

"It was a hasty marriage. We've really only known each other for two months. The first month through e-mail and phone calls."

"I would call that a hasty marriage."

"I shouldn't have said hasty," Caroline corrected herself. "Hasty makes it sound like it was a mistake."

The detective shook his head. "You just found out that your husband spent time in jail, that he lied to you about his identity and that he is now the prime suspect in a murder investigation, and you don't think the marriage was a mistake?"

Caroline didn't hesitate. "No, I don't."

He scowled but didn't respond. The officers searching the house returned with the computer from his downstairs office and nothing else.

"We'll be leaving now, but we'll be in touch."

"It doesn't make any sense," Caroline said. "Why would he kill Denny? Denny was his business. He made millions on his software programs. Isn't that a little like killing the goose that laid the golden egg?"

"Not if he thought he had enough eggs already," he answered. "We spent the morning with Steven Ford. It turns out that there is a discrepancy in the company's finances. Two million dollars appears to be missing."

Caroline shook her head angrily. "The company is worth ten times that. What does a man who is worth tens of millions of dollars need with two?"

"Good question. I'll be in touch."

Nora crouched in front of where Caroline sat. "I know this is going to be hard to believe, but if you know where he is you have to tell us. It's the only way we're going to figure this out. The only way, if he is innocent."

"He is."

"Then finding him is crucial to proving that."

"Who are you?" Caroline asked her. Her gut was screaming at her that something was off.

"I'm here at the request of the government. Encrypton was up for a big contract."

"No, I mean who are you?" Caroline pressed. "Are you... Do you know him? There was someone in the government. A former employee of his..."

"Hey, Agent FBI, you coming or not?" the detective called to her.

Nora took a card out of her purse along with a pen. She scribbled a number on the back of it. "This is my room number at the hotel where I'm staying." She added the name of the hotel to the card. "Call me. We'll talk. And Caroline, for what it's worth, the last thing he did before he left his office was look at your picture."

Caroline said nothing, but took the card and watched them leave. Munch followed them to the door and sounded off with a few harsh barks just to let them know she hadn't appreciated their company. Immediately she returned looking up at her mistress longingly. The question was easy to read in her confused eyes.

"I don't where he is," Caroline sobbed.

"What was that?" Mark wanted to know.

"What was what?" she asked as she followed him to his beige nondescript cop car. The siren light on top was the only thing that gave it a little character.

"You and the missus were getting pretty chummy."

"She's clearly distraught. You could have broken the news to her a little more gently."

Mark snorted. "I'm not in the nice business, shortcake. I'm trying to track a killer."

"A suspected killer. You keep forgetting that."

"Not you, though," Mark pointed out. "Don't tell me you think this guy is innocent?"

"I was trained not to form conclusions too early in an investigation."

"Well la-di-da," Mark sang. "I was trained to close cases. I've got a missing ex-con, who was one of two people who had access to books that were cooked, and a dead body. It seems pretty cut-and-dried to me."

"What about the wife's question? Why would a man already worth millions need to steal two?"

"I'm not sure about that," he admitted grudgingly. "It does sound a little weak."

"Maybe a little too cut-and-dried," she suggested.

"But that doesn't answer my question. Why are you rooting for the bad guy?"

She laughed. "I'm not rooting."

"You're rooting. Put a skirt on you and couple of pom-

poms in your hands and I would call you his personal cheerleading squad."

"I'm just here to observe and report back to Washington."

Mark accepted that for the time being. Only because he had to. At some point, though, he was going to have to do a little more digging into the pixie's story. She was cute, so he was really hoping his gut was off on this. But he didn't think so.

"I guess it sort of makes sense that Washington would want this guy to be clean. Otherwise they have to go looking for someone else."

They reached the car and he circled it to open the door for her. She looked at the open door, then at him.

"What? I can't be a gentleman?"

"It's just a little unexpected."

He smiled wolfishly. "Learn to expect the unexpected with me, shortcake."

Her eyes took on a decided glint. "Stop calling me short."

"Yes, sir, Agent FBI."

"You know, you could just call me Nora."

"I could but that wouldn't be as much fun."

She got into the car and he closed the door behind her. Then he circled around and got behind the wheel.

"So where to next?" he asked.

"I would like to see the crime scene if that's all right."

"Still don't trust me when I tell you that it was deliberate?" Mark asked.

"I want to see for myself," Nora said. Then she turned to him and smiled. "And for the record, I don't think I do trust you. You seem too eager to close this case and wash your hands of it."

"I'm crushed."

"Yeah, right."

He smiled again. "Okay, I'm not. For the record, I'm not so sure I trust you, either."

"That hurts not even a little bit."

"Wiseass." He started the car and reversed down the long driveway. The itchy edge overcame him and he felt his foot start to tap uncontrollably. It was hard to know if it was his passenger or… "On the way there though, we need to make a stop."

"Why?"

"I think my patch is wearing off."

Chapter 8

Caroline stood among the mourners and thought what a hypocrite she was. She didn't know this man. Had met him only once. She didn't know what his dreams or hopes had been. What used to make him laugh out loud or his favorite type of music. She only knew with every passing minute she had to suppress the urge to fling open the closed casket, haul his body out of it, shake him back to life and force him to admit who had done this to him.

Because it wasn't Dominic. It wasn't.

The minister Anne had arranged for said some final words. The small crowd, employees mostly and two police officers apparently sent by the detective to watch the proceedings, began to disperse. Caroline felt someone place an arm under her elbow and turned to find Steven trying to lead her away from the scene. She took one last look around, hoping much like she imagined the two officers were, to find Dominic hiding among the trees watching the service from a distance. A limo waited for them on the path that ran through the cemetery. Again, Anne's doing. They all climbed inside, Anne, her father, Steven and Caroline, as if they were members of Denny's immediate family.

Caroline supposed they were.

Without asking where they were going Caroline leaned her head back on the leather headrest and thought about the next step. Three days and there had been no word from Dominic. The police were still looking for him, of course, but Caroline had no expectation that Dominic would be found holed up in some seedy motel nearby.

He was too smart for that. Certainly he'd been smart enough to find a way to leave his past behind. He'd been smart enough to build a business. Smart enough to get her to the altar before she could think about what she was doing, thereby fulfilling his ultimate goal of securing a wife.

Yes, her husband was a very smart man.

But why? Why, if he was planning to kill off his partner, which she knew he hadn't done, would he have stopped to get married first? The police were considering that he acted spontaneously forcing Denny's car off the road. That whatever conversation they'd had the afternoon of Denny's death had triggered Dominic's violent intentions.

Then there were the employees who had come forward. Witnesses outside of Denny's office who heard raised voices coming from behind the closed door. Nothing specific. Just an increase in volume, according to what Hernandez told her.

Caroline tried to remember Dominic's mood when he'd come home that night. Something had been bothering him, but she hadn't pushed him on it because she was too wrapped up in her own pain.

But she knew that the only reason he'd gone to the office that night was because she sent him there. She'd backed him into a corner and he'd run. Could he have been planning to leave even before she confronted him?

No. He'd reached out to her. He'd wanted to make love. Make up. Could a man whose mind was on murder even get a hard-on?

Caroline huffed softly. Maybe she should take that to the police as proof of innocence.

The limo stopped. Startled Caroline looked up at the monstrosity that was her house.

"I thought I could put something together for lunch for us," Anne suggested. "We can talk. Brainstorm about where Dominic might be."

"Good luck with that, darling," Russell said but offered no reason for his skepticism. He exited the limo and offered a hand to his daughter.

Caroline felt Steven staring at her from the other seat. "We can leave. Give you time and space."

"To do what?" He remained silent. "Exactly. There is no answer to this, Steven. None. I go around and around and nothing makes sense."

"The answers are there. I know they are. I know that eventually Dominic will call us and tell us what happened. It can't end like this," he said tightly.

Feeling his frustration almost as keenly as her own Caroline reached out to pat his knee. "It's okay. Come inside. Serena sent over a ton of food. She doesn't know what to do now that she's not taking orders from Dominic. I imagine she thinks cooking for me is the next best thing."

They made their way inside and Caroline and Anne headed off to the kitchen to see about food and coffee.

"I can also put on some tea," Anne said, fidgeting

slightly with the single strand of pearls around her neck that complemented her simple black dress. "I don't know why, but anytime anything bad happens people always want to brew tea. You know? Like tea has some magical property to make everything go away."

Caroline reached out and laid her hand over Anne's. Immediately she stopped talking.

"I'm sorry. I'm babbling."

"Don't be," Caroline said. "You're worried and concerned. Just like the rest of us."

"Just like the rest of us."

Caroline paused for a second but decided she needed to know all the answers now. "Anne, what happened between you and Dominic?"

Immediately Anne snatched her hand away. She looked stunned, as if she'd just been slapped across the face. Caroline followed her gaze as she glanced over her shoulder, but the men had gone downstairs to Dominic's office. Probably to look through his files, his drawers. The police had already taken everything relating to the company. But maybe there was something left behind that Steven would recognize as being important.

"What are you saying?"

"Please. I'm not doing this to pry or bring up something embarrassing. But I need to know everything. Everything about Dominic that I didn't know before if I'm going to try and find him. At the party I felt as if there was something there. I don't know. A weird vibe."

Anne's shoulders slumped. Carefully she placed the two teacups she had in her hands on the counter. "That was my fault. I was trying too hard. It was a year ago. Steven was starting to talk about buying a piece of Encrypton. We were newly married, and let's say that I didn't take to it right away."

"I see."

"The truth is I'm spoiled," she chuckled humorlessly. "My daddy gave me everything I ever wanted. And part of what I love about Steven is that he doesn't. And part of what makes me furious with him is that he doesn't. I made a ridiculous pass at Dominic because I wanted to hurt Steven. Anyway, Dominic shot me down and that was the end of it. Since then I guess I've wanted to make sure we were friends. Good friends. So that hopefully he would forget what I did. That's what you saw at the party."

"Okay," Caroline said.

"It was a good party," Anne said, laughing softly without any humor. "I always throw great parties."

And despite knowing that she and Anne were never going to be bosom buddies, Caroline couldn't help but smile. Then another thought occurred to her. "You made a comment that day about how Dominic's marriage affected all of you. I didn't understand it then. Why would his marriage have anything to do with you?"

Anne grimaced. "I guess you're going to find out eventually. It's part of the business agreement, the way their partnership is structured. If anything happened to any one of them, then their piece of the company is left to the other partners. The only exception would be if they had children."

"I don't understand." But she was afraid she did.

"If something happened to Steven, then his share of the company reverts to Dominic. I would get a payout, but I couldn't own the company. Unless we had children. Then they would be entitled to their father's shares. I guess Denny and Dominic had a reason for it. And to buy in, Steven had to agree. I suppose they wanted to protect the business from moneygrubbing wives. Or maybe they just wanted to make sure that their vision was respected. Either way, the partners can only pass ownership to their children."

"*…I can give you what you want.*"

"*What I want?*"

"*A child. Your profile said you wanted children. You told me you considered having a child on your own…*"

The conversation came back to her immediately and she felt her stomach roll with nausea. When he told her that he had a legacy to leave his child, she had no idea how literally he meant it. Dominic wanted a child so he would have someone to inherit his company. Not because he wanted to be a father.

"You can't think…" Anne started, then stopped. Caroline registered the woman's sheepish expression and knew exactly where she was headed. Like a stewardess wordlessly pointing out the exits with two fingers. "I mean, it's not like he married you just for children. I can't see him being the type. Besides, if that was his only purpose he would have picked someone…"

"Younger." Caroline said calmly. "If Dominic wanted a guarantee of children, he could have found someone much younger than I am. He might have even insisted on fertility tests first. But he didn't." She wondered who she was trying to convince. "Besides, his reasons for marrying me have nothing to do with his supposed motives for killing Denny or for embezzling money from his own company. In fact, they contradict each other."

"That's why none of this makes sense," Anne agreed. "Nobody wins here."

"What happens if he does get caught?"

"If he gets caught, he goes to jail. He should have the sense to turn over his shares to Steven," Russell interrupted. The men, it seemed, had returned from their inspection of

Dominic's office. Russell stood with his arms crossed over his chest, obviously unashamed by his comments.

Steven appeared embarrassed. "It's not going to come to that, Russell. Dominic is innocent."

"Innocent of murder or embezzlement? Financial statements were altered."

"But the money wasn't stolen," Steven said to Caroline directly. "I checked our accounts. It's all there. Almost."

Caroline pounced. "Almost."

Steven pinched the bridge of his nose as if trying to stem a horrible headache. "Except ten thousand dollars. We had a petty cash account we kept on hand for miscellaneous expenses. Dominic withdrew the money that morning. After I told him what happened to Denny."

"There," Russell stated emphatically. "If that doesn't signal his guilt, I don't know what does. He planned to run. The bastard! He's put a viable company at risk. The jobs of a hundred people at stake."

"Oh, please, Russell," Steven stopped him with a raised hand. "You don't care about the employees of Encrypton. You care about your investment."

"Damn right I do. This is your future. And my daughter's, if you haven't forgotten. I'm not going to see everything I've risked ruined because of some convict who got it into his head to take the money and run. If he gets caught, he should give you the company. If he doesn't, you need to take legal action. We can still get that government contract. The product is good. The best on the market. Everything can be saved. But you need to act. And if you don't, I will."

"Daddy," Anne interjected, placing a hand on her father's arm. "Please. We're not there yet. Dominic will contact us. Soon. I know it." With her other hand, she reached out to touch Caroline's wrist.

Caroline looked down at the hand that held her. Anne was trying to offer comfort but Caroline didn't feel comforted. Looking at Russell's red face and Steven's clenched jaw, she realized that each of them had their reasons for being with her. And none of those reasons were concern for her welfare. Or for Dominic's.

"I don't know what to do," she whispered falling back against the counter feeling as if all her strength had left her.

"You?" Russell huffed. "Well, really, there's nothing for you to do. You don't have any vested interest in this company. Hell, you barely have any time invested in your marriage."

"That's enough, Russell," Steven snapped.

"I'm being practical. The marriage isn't legal. She has no say in what happens with the company." Russell faced her directly. "If I were you, I would leave. Cut your losses and go home."

Caroline thought about her house waiting for her back in Virginia. Her quiet life. Her small group of friends. How easy would it be to leave, to run home. Just like a coward.

She pushed herself off the counter and moved away from the three of them. "I am home. And I think you should leave."

"Caroline, Daddy didn't mean…"

"I know what he meant. I'm not even saying he's wrong for thinking it. You believe Dominic is guilty."

"Damn right I do."

"Then we're at odds. I believe he's innocent. You should leave."

Russell took a step toward her, his gaze suspicious. "If you think that there is any loophole, any way for you to get your hands on this company, think again, little lady."

"I don't want the company," she said quietly, unflustered by Russell's threatening tone. "I want my husband back."

"Let's just go," Steven said. His shoulders slumped and Caroline could see the exhaustion in his face. It seemed he hadn't slept any more in the last few days than she had. Steven stood back as Russell took Anne's hand and led her out the front door. When they were beyond earshot he grasped Caroline's hand.

"We're not at odds. I don't think he's guilty, either."

Caroline said nothing.

"But if he contacts you in any way, you have to let me know. He has to come back from wherever the hell he is hiding and make this right. My father-in-law is a greedy money-hungry bastard, but he's got a point. We still have a chance to save this contract. More than that, this company needs Dominic. It *is* Dominic. Without him, I don't know."

"Okay." It was an easy reply that answered nothing. But Steven must have seen in her face that she wasn't going to say anything else. After a moment, he left and followed his family outside.

The door closed behind him and for a while Caroline stared at it, thinking about what came next. The funeral was over. The murder investigation was proceeding. Dominic was out there somewhere…doing what? Hiding? Or maybe searching for Denny's killer on his own.

What was her next move? She could look for him. Drive around Half Moon Bay calling out his name as if he were a lost dog but what was the point?

Suddenly feeling as exhausted as Steven looked, she climbed the stairs and found Munch waiting for her on the bed. The dog lifted her head as if to offer an invitation and Caroline took her up on it. She dropped down on Dominic's side and tried to remember what it felt like to lie next to him. To smell him. To hear him breathe.

Tears rolled into her hair, but before she could work up the energy to wipe them away she drifted off into a dreamless sleep.

The sound of a loud ringing woke her up. Startled, she jerked into consciousness. A second later, she recognized the sound of the phone. The room was dark, dusk having long since passed, but she had no problem finding the phone on the bedside table. It was the same one she'd picked up when Steven called her that fateful morning.

"Hello?" she answered as she sat up. Her voice was rusty with sleep so she tried again when she got no answer. "Hello?"

"Go home."

Confused by the response, it took a second for Caroline to recognize the dark voice.

"Dominic!"

"Go home." Click.

The dial tone echoed in her ear. Then later, the sound of a busy signal indicating the phone had been off the hook too long shook her out of her daze.

It was him. His voice. His words. His order. There was no way to mistake it for anything else.

Go home.

She wanted to scream at him. If he'd been standing in front of her, she would have chucked the phone at him.

Go *home?* She was home. This was home. This was where she was supposed to be! Wasn't it? Cut your losses. That's what Russell had said. And if Dominic didn't want her to stay…

What was the point of hanging on if the person you were hanging on for was willing to let you go?

"Munch," Caroline said calmly. "We're leaving."

Chapter 9

"I'm leaving."

Caroline stood in the area marked off in the San Jose police headquarters as Mark Hernandez's office. An area that consisted of a desk and a chair.

"When was the last time you slept for more than three hours?"

It wasn't the response she was expecting.

"Did you hear what I said?"

"I heard it. I just don't get it."

"I talked to my lawyer back home. I'm from Virginia. He said you can't hold me here if I'm not a person of interest."

The detective shrugged. "He's right. But why now? Last time we talked, you seemed pretty convinced your man was going to come back and that he was innocent."

"He is innocent."

"So why are you leaving now?"

Because even though he was innocent, he wasn't coming back. At least not for her. "I…I just have to," she stumbled.

"Caroline, I'm going to ask you a question and I need you to answer me honestly. Has Dominic Santos been in touch with you?"

"No." She didn't feel guilty about lying to the police— she felt stupid. Stupid that even though Dominic had crushed her heart with his brief order, she was still doing everything she could to protect him. She took out a card and passed it to the detective. "That's all my information if you need to get in touch with me for any reason."

"You're leaving?" Caroline turned around and saw the FBI agent from the other day walking toward her. Again she was struck by a sense of familiarity that she couldn't place.

"I am."

"Don't do this, Caroline. He'll turn up. Eventually."

Caroline tried to smile through the crush of tears. "That's not good enough. I can't think. I can't stop worrying. How did this happen? I had no one. And I took this chance. Then suddenly I was happy. One phone call and it was all gone. I have no idea if he's coming back. Should I get over him? Fight for him? I haven't a clue. You don't know me. I'm not brave enough for any of this." She took a deep breath and then another. "You can't make me stay."

"Nobody is forcing you to stay, Caroline," Nora said. "I just think you're kidding yourself if you think you're going to worry less or be less sad in Virginia. Also I think you're wrong. Maybe I don't know you very well, but you seem pretty brave to me."

"I have to go." She turned back to the detective. "You know how to reach me if he does come back."

"I'll call."

* * *

Nora watched Caroline turn and leave the station. Walking so carefully, as if she had to concentrate on each step or else she would stumble and fall.

"Something happened."

"Yep. That's my guess, too. But she wouldn't cop to it. It's probably for the best she's leaving," Mark commented.

"How do you figure?"

"Why get dragged down with him? The guy lied to her. The marriage wasn't legal. And she only knew him for a couple of months. At this point she can cut her losses and move on with her life."

Nora shook her head at him, clearly disgusted. "Can't you see that she's in love?"

Mark laughed. "You're kidding me, right?"

Nora scowled at him. "No, I'm not kidding. What's so funny about that?"

"Love at first sight. Bullshit. Hormones at first sight, I'll buy. But nobody should be shackled with a criminal for a husband for the rest of her life just because of hormones."

"Would it be terribly cliché of me right now to huff, stomp my foot, and say, *Men!*"

"Yep."

"Then I'll pass. Tell me about the money. The ten thousand dollars."

Back to business, Mark acknowledged. Actually, it's part of what he liked about Nora. She had the same no-nonsense approach to work as he did. She knew when to play, but she also knew when to get serious. Unlike most federal types who were always just serious.

The other part he liked about her was that strange and intriguing mark on her nose. What the hell was that? Oh, and her lips. They were big and full and made a man want to bite them. But he would keep that information to himself until after the case was wrapped up.

Business first. Pleasure right after that. It was his personal motto.

"Bank records show him withdrawing ten thousand dollars from the company's checking account at exactly 9:02 on the morning he learned of Denny's murder. Seems like a pretty suspicious thing to do, doesn't it?"

"Not if you think you need to run. Dominic is a smart man. If he was going to run, he knew he'd require money to do it. The real question is if he is innocent, why did he think he needed to take off?"

"How do you know Santos is a smart man?"

Nora blinked. "He owns a multimillion dollar software company. It's not a job for dummies. He figured out how to lose his past. Also not easy for the mentally challenged. This is a smart guy we're dealing with. You're dealing with. It's why you haven't found him yet."

Mark snorted. "Right."

"What did you think I meant?"

"I don't know," he said casually. "Sounds like you've gone from cheerleader to gaga over this guy. Almost like you know him."

"I read an article about him in *Software Digest* once. He seemed…interesting."

"So that's what this is," Mark said telling himself he was not jealous. No way.

"What?"

"You've got a crush on this guy."

Nora rolled her eyes. "You're a jackass."

"Not disputing that. But I'm right. So you're a computer geek…"

"Watch it," she growled.

"Computer lady?"

"Better."

"And he owns a software company. Is he, like, your idol? Tell me, do you carry his picture around in your wallet?"

"Drop it, Detective," Nora told him. "My point is still a valid one. He's smart, he's on the run and now we know he's got enough cash to hide out for a while."

"He's got enough cash to be in Mexico right now drinking mai-tais on a beach. He didn't get his hands on the two million, but that doesn't mean he doesn't have some other money stashed away. Hell, he's probably got bank accounts all over the damn world. We're never going to find this guy."

Nora plopped herself down in the seat across from him. She crossed her legs, which made the slim navy skirt she was wearing ride up her legs slightly. Mark stared at the three-inch heels stabbing into space and wondered how she walked on the suckers without falling off. Jeez, she turned him on.

"It doesn't make sense."

"It makes perfect sense," Mark insisted.

"If this is just about the money, why settle for two million when he's worth considerably more?"

"Maybe he was tired of the rat race."

"So why not sell his share of the company?" Nora said.

Mark thought about that. "Maybe there is something wrong with the company. Santos knew and he was jumping ship before it all came crashing down around him. Figured he'd leave it to the partners to clean up the mess."

"I suppose that could work."

Mark's smile was feral. "I'm good."

"If you're so good, then tell me this. Why does a man, who knows his company is about to crumble, who is prepared to embezzle money and ditch, suddenly decide to get married? You know about the partnership agreement?"

"The what?"

"The three partners. I talked to the company's attorney regarding Denny's assets. He told me that his share of the business reverts back to Santos and Ford. He said that in the event of something happening to any of them, only their children would inherit. Children none of them has. Seems to me like a man who decides to get married is thinking about the future."

Damn.

Nora lifted her hands in the air. "Sorry. You can't have it both ways. You already said he couldn't have married for love."

"He could have married for hormones."

"He could have just slept with her to satisfy his hormones. He didn't have to marry her. No, he wanted something with her. A future. Kids. Somebody he could leave everything that he'd worked for. Doesn't sound like he thought his company was in trouble. Which gets us back to why a man in his position decides to embezzle from his own business."

"Unless he didn't do it," Mark finished.

"Unless he didn't do it," Nora repeated. "Let's consider another option."

The phone on his desk rang and he scowled at her, mostly because he hated to be wrong.

"What?" he snapped into the phone. "Yeah. Yeah. Huh. Okay." He hung up the phone and considered the information he'd just heard.

"So?"

"We got the security tapes from the office the night Haskell died."

Nora waited for a beat. "And you're building up the suspense here because…"

Because things were starting to get all sorts of murky. Mark didn't like murky. He liked nice and simple. Bad guys, good guys. Innocent. Guilty. You find the guy who did it and you put him in jail. Then you win the girl and take her to bed.

"The tapes show that Santos showed up about midnight. Then about an hour later, Haskell left alone. The camera in the garage shows him getting into his Porsche and driving off. A few minutes later, a Mercedes, same model as Santos's, with tinted windows, drives past a camera and leaves the garage."

Nora sat up straighter in the hard metal chair.

"The tire treads taken from the scene match the brand of tire typically sold on a Mercedes."

"Really," Nora muttered. "So why do you look so unhappy?"

"Because the only tape we have of Santos leaving the building is at 5:00 a.m. the next morning. Walking out through the lobby."

"Hmm."

Mark looked up at Nora. Saw the obvious confusion in her face. "It's not out of the question that he knew how to get in and out of the building without being picked up by the cameras. He's an ex-con, remember? He knows how to be careful."

"But he didn't think of that when he drove by a camera to follow Haskell?"

"It's the only way out of the garage."

"You said he walked out the next morning. No car. You haven't found the Mercedes?"

"No."

"If he used it to push Denny's Porsche off the road, the likelihood is that he would have dumped the car somewhere."

Mark agreed.

"Let's play it out. We know Haskell and Santos argued about something that afternoon. Santos goes back to the office again and Denny is there. They continue their earlier battle. Maybe Haskell found out about the altered financial statements. Quickly Santos decides he has to kill him. He sneaks out of the building without being picked up by the cameras, then manages to get to his car without being seen…"

"That's conceivable," Mark interrupted. "The garage is the first floor of the building. It wouldn't be hard for someone to get over the wall and drop into the garage out of sight of the cameras. There's only one at the elevator and one at the entrance and exit."

"Okay, so he sneaks out of the building and back into the garage in time to follow his target. Then he tails him for what thirty, forty minutes?"

Mark mentally timed the drive from the office to the spot on the cliff where Denny went over the edge. "About right."

"Pushes him off the road and over the cliff. There has to be a mark on his car. Paint scratches, something. So he dumps the car. Where?"

"Who knows? Down the road a ways. Over another cliff."

"This would mean he would have to have had another car waiting to take him back to the office, which eliminates our idea that it was a spur of the moment decision. He couldn't walk back and be there in time to take Steven's four-thirty call. Maybe he phoned for a cab. They keep logs."

"I'll check with cab companies."

"Or he drove back to San Jose and dumped the car somewhere close to the office. Then he snuck back into the building again without being seen. We have to assume he's really rattled at this point, which is why he doesn't destroy the doctored books. They're the only motive we have for why he might have killed Denny. I mean he was sitting in front of his computer when Ford called. We know he checked the financials. Yeah, he was definitely flustered."

Mark sneered at her. "You know, I don't think I like you anymore."

"Yes you do," she said cheekily. "You should concentrate your search for the car in the area around the office building. Because it will be there somewhere if Santos is your guy."

Mark frowned. What she laid out made perfect sense. Perfectly convoluted sense. But the biggest problem Mark had was digesting the fact that someone who had made the decision to kill as quickly as Dominic managed to pull it off so flawlessly.

"You know all he's going to need for an alibi is proof that he was still in the building at the time Denny's car was going over the cliff. A phone call. An e-mail. The computer time-stamps them." Nora leaned back in the chair.

"The forensic guys are checking out his computer. And we're waiting on the phone company for calls from the office as well as Santos's cell and Haskell's cell." Mark pointed a finger at her. "You know, if I didn't know you better…"

"You don't know me at all, Detective."

"I'm getting to," Mark assured her. "I would say you seem almost smug. It's like you know this guy is innocent and you're just waiting for us to find that out."

"How could that be?"

"Good question. Got an answer?"

Nora checked her fingernails. "Nope. I told you I'm just here to observe and report back to my superiors."

"That is what you told me."

Nora feigned offense. "Why Detective, I think I'm insulted. I believe you're insinuating that I'm not being completely forthcoming."

"Oh, not at all. I'm calling you an out-and-out liar." He got up from his desk. "I've got other cases that need my attention. Until I hear back from the phone company or unless our guy shows up, there's really no need for you to hang around here."

Nora stood up, too. "First you call me a liar and now you're kicking me out," she grumbled. "What am I supposed to do in the meantime?"

"Go sightseeing, shortcake."

"Have I not warned you about the 'short' thing?"

"I like to live dangerously," he said and waved to her as she snatched up her purse and strolled out of the police station.

As soon as he saw the glass doors close behind her, he reached for his phone.

Chapter 10

Caroline dropped her suitcase inside the foyer of her dark house and felt Munch brush past her as the dog went in search of new smells. The trip had been one of the most excruciating ordeals of her life. Between the guilt she felt in leaving, the anger she felt at being told to go and getting a one-hundred-pound-plus Lab across the country, she was spent.

Looking down at the lone suitcase she'd quickly packed, she wondered if she would ever go back for the rest of her things. Wondered if he would ever come for Munch. She tried to tell herself that her only option was to take his dog. After all, who else would care for her? Caroline had easily dismissed his dog sitter as an option because she wanted Munch with her. It was only fair.

He broke her heart. She took his dog.

Relationship justice.

The laptop joined the suitcase with about as much

ceremony. The story she had barely started was tucked safely inside, but she had no interest in working on it. It was a murder mystery and the sleuths were a husband and wife. When she'd conceived it she'd played with the idea of turning the book into a series.

Now the story of a husband and wife investigating a murder was too nonfiction for her tastes. She would write again. Wouldn't she? Caroline decided not to answer the question while her mental battery was giving her the low-power warning.

A week. She would give it a week and then she would miss him a little less. In a month and she might look back on all of this and realize she'd made a fortuitous escape. Perhaps in a year she'd find the humor…

No. She'd never laugh about her marriage.

Leaving the bags where they were, she headed upstairs. There was no point in flicking a light switch as she'd had the electricity turned off weeks ago. As familiar as she was with the house, she knew her way around in the dusk. Fall was hitting the east coast at a rapid rate if the orange and red leaves were any indication. Just past seven in the evening there was enough light to guide her up the stairs and down the hall to the room that had been her bedroom for so many years.

Caroline knew she'd stripped the bed before she'd locked up the house but she would find what she needed in the linen closet. Some sheets. A familiar blanket. A soft pillow.

Sleep first and think later. Eventually she and Munch would need to eat, but not for a while. In a few hours she could deal with having to move back into her empty home. In a few hours she might be able to concentrate on something other than the empty space in her soul.

A soft *roof* behind her had her jumping a bit as Munch

rushed past her up the stairs. Having apparently sniffed out the downstairs she was ready to tackle the second floor. Caroline climbed the last step when she heard a sharp bark from one of the guest rooms.

This bark wasn't a curious smell bark. It was an *I found something* bark.

No doubt a squirrel or raccoon or some other small animal had made its way into the empty house looking for warmth as temperatures started to dip. The idea of summoning the energy to get the thing out of the house was so daunting that she began to think about leaving and crashing at her neighbor's. But facing her friends meant answering questions and she didn't want to do that, either.

Another bark. This one even louder.

"What is it, Munch? Is it a squirrel? Don't be afraid. Remember, you're bigger." Caroline rounded the doorway prepared to deal with the furry intruder when the shift of a shadow stopped her heart.

Too big. Too big to be an animal.

As soon as the thought registered, she turned to run. An arm snaked out and caught her around the waist hauling her backward against a large hard body. Another hand circled her mouth cutting off her attempt to scream. Not that she had the air left to make any sound.

Then a voice. Rough and soft in her ear. His voice. "Don't scream. I won't hurt you."

Her last thought before she drifted away into oblivion was that he already had.

The first thing that registered was the feel of the washcloth on her brow. A memory of when she'd first come to this house, after her parents' funeral, surfaced. Caroline had cried herself sick that day until finally she'd collapsed with exhaustion. Her aunt had washed her face with a cold washcloth to ease the swelling around her eyes. She could almost hear the soft voice telling her everything was going to be all right.

But that was years ago. This was now.

Caroline opened her eyes and screamed.

Instantly a hand dropped over her mouth and a large and heavy body followed. She felt crushed by him. In the pitch black she couldn't see his eyes, could only make out the harsh lines of his face. Her breath was trapped in her lungs and she struggled to shake him off.

Dominic was an immovable object on top of her.

Her legs brushed against his jean-covered thighs and only then did she realize that he'd removed her clothes. She was wearing nothing but her shirt and panties. Her sense of vulnerability increased and so did her struggles.

"Stop it," Dominic whispered in her ear.

Caroline relaxed her body, not because of his demand but because there was no point in trying to move him. She lay motionless and felt every inch of his body against hers. Including his erection that was pressing into her stomach.

"If I take my hand away, you can't scream. Your neighbors are close and I don't want to take the chance of them hearing anything."

She nodded. Eventually he rolled away and quickly left the bed. His back was to her as he checked outside her window looking for any disturbances. Eventually he turned and walked toward her. When she slid away from him to the center of the bed, he stopped.

"You're frightened," he said to himself in a disgusted tone.

He lit a candle on the nightstand and sat on the edge of the bed. It seemed as if he was waiting for her to make the next move.

She had no clue how to react. "I don't know what to say to you, Dominic."

"Then don't say anything," he replied. "You're exhausted. You fainted."

"I didn't faint." Fainting sound so weak. So out of control. Cowards fainted. And she couldn't have the conversation she needed to have with him if she was a coward.

"I scared you. I'm sorry. There is nothing to be afraid of."

She couldn't name the emotion that she was feeling right now. Strangely it wasn't fear. Rage, maybe. Pain. Sorrow. And, damn it, hope.

She was an idiot.

"Why? I mean… What? I don't…"

"Shh," he said again. Two fingers covered her lips in a request to silence her. Even after everything that had happened, her heart fluttered at his touch. The urge to purse her lips and kiss those fingers was almost irresistible. "I'll answer everything. I promise, Caroline. But not now. You need to sleep."

"I can't."

"Please," he asked or ordered, it was hard to know. He nudged her over more toward the center. She watched as he stood and kicked off his sneakers and pulled off his T-shirt.

She wanted to tell him to stop. That she didn't want to even look at him much less sleep with him, she was so angry. But in the candlelight, his movements seemed a little stilted and she decided he was just as tired as she was.

She knew he wasn't a murderer. She had no idea what his other crime had been, but he'd never hurt her. It was probably insane, but she didn't have the words to stop him.

Not that it would have mattered. He lay down on his side next to her and he pulled her body into his chest. She smelled the faint hint of soap and the full-on scent of

Dominic. The comfort she felt as his arms wrapped around her and a leg settled between hers was enough to bring tears to her eyes.

"I can't do this," she cried softly, struggling a little against his hold.

His arms tightened and his lips pressed against her temple. "Shh, shh. It's going to be all right. Later. I'll answer everything later. I promise. Sleep with me now, Caroline. It's been so long since I've slept. I need you to just sleep with me for a while. Then we'll talk."

She could hear the plea in his voice and it stopped her internal struggles more than anything else. The idea that he would verbalize any weakness was new to her. She suspected it was new to him, as well. Already she could feel the rise and fall of his chest. The sound of steady breathing in her ear.

There was no way she was going to sleep. There were too many things to think about, too many questions she needed to prepare for him to answer. But they could wait. For now, he needed some rest.

Closing her eyes, she tried to think about everything she had to ask him, but the heat from his body made her drowsy and the soft rumble of his snore made her mind wander. With his hand pressed against her heart, she fell asleep, too.

The sound of a steady rain hitting against the glass woke him. The dull light outside the window told him it was early morning. They had slept for almost twelve hours.

He turned his head and studied the face that lay against his shoulder. He could feel the warm breath hitting his skin and his world came back into focus. If he could have shouted his relief he would have. With a finger, he brushed a lock of blond hair from her forehead and traced the insignificant line in her brow, one that had probably deepened in the last few days with worry.

God, he'd missed her. There was no point denying it. Yes, it wasn't supposed to be like this. Their marriage was supposed to have been an arrangement. A sensible, logical business transaction. But from the first glance at her picture, the first e-mail, the first time he heard her voice and the first time he sank his body deep into hers, he knew.

She was different.

He wondered if she would remember one of the last things she'd said to him was that she was falling in love. He remembered. It stayed with him every hour of every day. It kept him moving and plotting for a way out of this mess.

He had no illusions that her feelings would still be what they were now that she knew about his past, but he wasn't ready to let her go. Somehow he'd made her fall in love with him once. If she let him try, maybe he could do it again.

As if hearing his thoughts, Caroline blinked her eyes open.

Their eyes met and the silent communication was so intense he was sure he could hear her speaking. He wondered if she could hear him in return.

You need a shave.

Thank you for taking care of Munch.

I missed you.

Yes.

Without thinking, Dominic leaned forward until their lips met. He pulled her deeper against his body and wondered if he would have the power to let her go if she resisted him.

She didn't. Instead he felt her arm around his back, felt her mouth open beneath his so that he could taste her, penetrate her, breathe her in.

He'd missed her. So damn much. He wanted to be inside

her so she would absorb the pain. Replace it with pleasure. He wanted to erase Denny. He didn't want to grieve his loss. Didn't want to be frustrated or angry anymore because someone had done this to him. He didn't want to be afraid any longer.

And he was frightened. Frightened he was going to lose this. Lose her.

The kiss deepened and Dominic rolled onto his back, taking her with him. Her legs tangled with his thighs and he wished he'd shucked his pants as well as his shirt so that he could feel her soft thighs against him. He cupped her bottom and pulled her close against his hard sex and her hand rested over his heart.

He knew she could feel his body pounding, throbbing underneath his skin, and he was glad. He needed her to know how desperately he wanted her. How he had never wanted another woman like this before.

Then the hands that rested on his chest began to push instead of caress.

"No, I can't do this. I'll forget," Caroline muttered pulling away from him, lifting out of his arms.

Dominic sighed and let his head drop against the pillow. He was desperate to stop her from moving away. A quick jerk of her wrist and she'd be stretched out flat against his chest. Another twist and he'd have her on her back. A button undone and a lowered zipper and he'd be pushing inside her warmth.

With everything he'd learned about her in the last month, he could woo her. Seduce her. Prove to her that their connection was special and could survive anything. He could win back her love.

If not her trust.

Selfish. He wasn't thinking about her at all, really. Just himself. Just that he needed her. She had a right to back away.

Hell, she could walk out the front door and call the police if she chose. And as much as the idea of the police made him sweat cold, he knew he wouldn't stop her. The next move was hers. Her call to do whatever she wanted because none of this, not from the first moment he'd signed up with that damn matchmaking service because he needed an incubator for his child, had been her fault.

He thought about what he had to tell her and wondered how much of his soul he was going to have to lay at her feet to make her believe him.

She rolled off him and stood next to the bed. Her arms crossed over her chest, she lowered her head. His eyes were still drawn to her bare legs that he knew from experience could tighten around his waist like a vise when she was excited.

He waited for the questions to start. He figured she would begin with the obvious and ask him if he was a murderer. Or maybe she would want to know about his past first. His criminal record.

Instead, she took him completely by surprise.

Chapter 11

"Why did you leave me?"

His throat closed and he needed to swallow before he could answer. Pushing himself off the bed, he stood on the other side of it across from her. Munch, who had been sleeping soundly at the foot of the bed, was suddenly awake. She looked from master to mistress, clearly torn in her loyalties.

"Downstairs, Munch." The dog immediately obeyed scampering off to do more exploring. Dominic was struck with the silly idea that he didn't want the dog to see her parents fighting.

"Why?" Caroline asked again. This time her voice was tighter, angrier.

"I had to," he answered simply even though he knew that there was nothing simple about it. He tried to pull his thoughts, put them into some kind of chronological order that would make sense. He wasn't the damn storyteller.

She was shaking her head, "If you're not going to give me more than that, I'm leaving. I mean it."

Leaving had the necessary effect. "I knew I had been set up. Knew it wouldn't be long before the police found out who I was. I didn't have enough time."

"Time to do what?" she pressed.

"Time to figure out what the hell had happened to Denny!" He took a breath and ran a hand through his hair as everything came back to him again. "After you and I argued that night, I went to the office. Denny was there. We had talked that afternoon. He told me what he was working on."

"You said it was dangerous."

"Yes. Anyway, that wasn't all and for whatever reason, he decided he didn't want any more secrets between us."

"What's wrong with Denny's project?"

"It's trouble. Bad trouble," Dominic elaborated. "Over-our-head trouble. Nothing that I wanted for Encrypton, I can promise you that. I told him to go home. That I would contact some people. And he left. Alive. You have to know that, Caroline. You have to believe I didn't kill him."

"I do."

That was it. Two words, and all the fear and worry and anguish he'd felt in the last week was suddenly gone. Two words, and he had hope his life wasn't over. Two words, and she'd sealed her fate as much as when she'd spoken those same words in front of the justice of the peace. Because he was never going to let her go.

Caroline was standing across from him. She was safe. She was with him. And she believed him. Nothing else mattered.

Breathing slowly, letting her belief in him settle inside his gut, he was able to tell her everything that had happened from the moment he'd learned of Denny's project.

"It was late. My mind was racing. I sent an e-mail to

a contact in Washington. With the time difference, I didn't
expect an answer right away, but I was too keyed up to
even think about leaving. I don't know what compelled
me to stay. It was work and I was there. I needed to
review the financial statements before our meeting next
month. Files that were on my hard drive. There were
entries against an expense account to a vendor I knew we
didn't have."

"Two million dollars' worth."

"You know." She nodded and it made sense. The police
would have needed something beyond his record as a
reason for killing Denny. Money was the motive. A
perfect setup. "I knew it couldn't be anything but deliberate. Someone had gotten on to my system and replaced
real financials with the altered ones. Then Steven called
with the news that Denny had been killed and suddenly
it made sense."

"It made sense?" Caroline sounded surprised. "You just
heard that your partner was forced off a cliff and that made
sense to you?"

"You have to understand the nature of the software
program he designed and its implications. If what he told
me is true, then I can think of hundreds, maybe thousands
of people who would be desperate to get their hands on it."

"But who else knew what he was working on?"

"I don't know." Dominic shrugged. "I asked him if he told
anyone else about it. He said he hadn't, but he was lying."

"How do you know?"

"I knew Denny. He couldn't lie worth shit. Lying is a
communication skill and he didn't have any. I didn't press
him because I thought we had time. I figured I could call
in the cavalry before it got out of hand. I was wrong.
Whoever he told killed him and set me up. When I left the

building and saw that my car was gone, I knew it had been the one used to push Denny off the road."

"Why didn't you go to the police? Tell them."

"I'm an ex-con!" Dominic shouted, the frustration he'd felt those hours after Denny's death resurfacing. "You know that now. I would have had to tell them everything. Who I was, my past, everything. Some detective would have shown up, seen the missing money, a Mercedes with a few dents in it, and an ex-con with a forged identity. They would have had me in jail so fast it would have made your head spin."

Her jaw tightened and her lips pressed firmly together. He felt guilty for shouting at her and wanted to take it back. But he was afraid if he reached out to her, she would pull away from him. It would kill him.

"We could have proved your innocence," she said softly. "You didn't do it so there will be proof. The e-mail you sent to your contact in Washington. That alone could be enough of an alibi. What did you think running would get you?"

Dominic turned away from her and sat on the bed. He stared out the window that overlooked her small patch of backyard. He saw a section of it that had been roped off and realized she must have had a garden at one point. He imagined her kneeling in the dirt, a big hat on her head to protect her from the sun, plucking a misshapen tomato. A sweet picture. How was he ever going to make someone like that understand what prison had done to him?

He heard her move around the bed and then she was standing over him. Her hand resting on his shoulder. The warmth of that touch spread to his toes.

"Talk to me."

He shook his head. "I couldn't risk it. I couldn't risk spending a day in jail. Being in a cage almost destroyed me. And I knew if I saw one close on me again, I would lose it. Totally lose it. Yes, I sent the e-mail, but I don't know when Denny's car went off the road. I was alone in an empty office. There was motive. I couldn't risk it."

"Okay."

He looked up at her. "Okay? That's it. You accept that as an answer." Because it was a lousy answer. Even he knew it. He just didn't have the vocabulary to explain what going back to jail would have done to him.

She cupped his face in her hand. "Do you think I shouldn't?"

"It's the only answer I have."

"Then it's enough."

"Because you love me," he realized. The power of it was astounding. He wondered what the one thing in his life was that he'd done right to deserve this woman and her faith in him.

Sighing, Caroline dropped on the bed next to him. Her hip bumped up against his. From the moment she'd met him, every action she'd taken had been rash, illogical and so against her natural inclinations to stay safely tucked away that she almost questioned her sanity. However, there wasn't one thing she regretted.

"Tell me I'm not a fool."

His laugh was quick, almost harsh. "I wish I could. I wish I could tell you that loving me made sense, but it doesn't, Caroline. I have done nothing to deserve you but I know if you got up from this bed and ran out of the house I would follow you to the ends of the earth and drag you back to me."

"That's good to know. It doesn't mean that you get a blank check, though. I still need answers and I'll know if you're lying. You're not the best at it, either. You get this red flush on your cheeks. It's a pretty bad tell."

He pulled her hand against his face and held it against his traitorous cheek. "Thank you."

"We're not done yet." She looked around the bare room. "When did you come back here?"

"I withdrew ten thousand dollars out of a miscellaneous account and got on a plane heading east before the police actively started looking for me. This was the first place I thought of. I broke in through the back door. The lock is pathetic, by the way. Before we leave, we'll need to replace it."

Replace the lock. Funny. It was such a husbandly thing to say.

"I lit candles when I needed them and snuck out every once in a while for food. And I waited. I waited as long as I could."

Caroline was about to ask him what he'd been waiting for when suddenly it occurred to her that the reason she was here with him now was because he'd called her.

Go home. Go home.

He hadn't been sending her away. He had called her to him. A giddy feeling filled her heart. "You knew. You knew if you told me to leave that I would have no choice but to come back here. You wanted me to come!"

He gripped her hand. "Wanted? I was desperate. Someone set me up. Someone killed Denny. Someone who had access to the company financials, my computer, my car. Someone who knew about my past. There is a murderer back there. A murderer who knows me. Knows you. I had to get you out of there."

"A murderer," she repeated. It was a word she'd used so blithely in her books. A bad guy. A character with means and motive and lacking morals. She'd fictionally bumped off people a dozen different ways, but now it was real.

Someone had killed Denny. Someone Dominic knew. Someone she knew. My God.

"I realized if I called too soon the police might think it was suspicious you leaving so quickly. But after a few days, well, you had no real ties to me. Leaving might be a logical thing for you to do. I waited as long I could, every day sick to death, afraid for you. I also knew you were the only person I could trust."

No. Not the only one. "Tell me about the contact in Washington."

Dominic shook his head "She's gone. I don't know where. I don't even know if she got my message. We can't count on her."

"I think you're wrong. I think you can," Caroline said slowly. "She's the former employee. Your contact in D.C."

"Yes."

"Who is she?" Caroline continued. "I mean, other than an FBI agent by the name of Eleanor Rodgers."

His body jerked. "How do you know her?"

"She's in San Jose. Right now. She came to the house with the detective in charge of the case. She said she was there as an observer. She gave me her card and said if there was anything I needed to contact her. I felt like…I felt like she was on my side. Which didn't make any sense to me, but I was a little distracted at the time. Who is she?"

"She used to work for me at Encrypton. She had some trouble with the law as a juvenile, but she had an amazing talent for computers. I gave her a chance, got her a decent education. A few years ago, she was recruited by the FBI. She believes she owes me. I knew I could trust her and more than that, I knew she would immediately understand the implications of Denny's program."

Caroline studied his face while he spoke. He wasn't

lying. At least she didn't think he was. But the distance was back. It was there in the formality of his words. As if he was picking and choosing them carefully. She'd teased him about the flush on his cheeks, but the truth was she didn't need that to know when he wasn't telling her everything.

"You're lying," she accused him. "There's more. Was she your lover?"

"No," he said.

"Then what?" Caroline's mind searched for an answer that made sense. If Nora wasn't a former lover, why would he hide the truth about who she was? An image of the woman's face flashed in her mind. She recalled her dark feathery hair and brown eyes, and remembered thinking that she looked familiar.

"Why does it matter?"

"Because you need my help," Caroline reminded him. "Because in order for me to give you that help, I have to trust you. Completely. I can't do that when you hold back. I would shake it out of you if I could, but you're too damn big. So I'm telling you it ends now. You have to let me in."

"You are in," he said tightly.

"No, it's not enough. You think you've let me inside, but you don't realize how many levels of defense you have."

"I'm trying."

It was barely a whisper, but it gave her hope. "I know. Who is she?"

He paused. "She's my half sister."

It was the truth. "You told me you had no family."

"She's my father's daughter. He abandoned her like he did me. Only her mother was lucky. She remarried. Nora's stepfather adopted her, but they never got along. As a teenager she had an attitude. Revenge, spite, who knows why a teenager does what she does? She went looking for her real father only to be told by him that he wanted nothing to do with her."

Caroline tightened her grip on his hand in a knee-jerk reaction of sympathy for a girl who was all grown up. "How did she find you?"

"Like I said, she had a talent with computers. Somehow she tracked me down. Found me despite my new identity." Dominic grinned as he remembered. "She showed up in my office with spiked purple hair, white face paint, chains from one end of her body to the other, combat boots and a ring through her nose. I thought she was from the circus, but she told me who she was and threatened to expose my past if I didn't give her the money she needed to run away."

"You gave her a job instead."

"Then I called her mother."

Of course he did. Caroline swallowed the lump in her throat as it once more became painfully obvious to her that this man, her husband, was a good guy.

"Nora and I aren't close. My fault. She tried a couple of times, but I did everything I could to keep her at a distance. She could work for me, but I didn't let her stay in my house. I didn't acknowledge to anyone that she was related to me. She was an employee. That's all."

"You regret that."

He nodded. "I went to see her graduate from the academy. She didn't know I was there. I thought if we got this government contract I would be traveling back and forth to D.C. a lot. I thought maybe I could try to see her. Get to know her."

Caroline rested her head on his shoulder. "You're really pathetic, you know that?" She felt him flinch, but he didn't pull away. "You did everything you could to keep this person out, too. But the second you sent her an e-mail saying you needed help, she was on the first flight out to the west coast. You know, for someone who does everything he can to keep people at arm's length, you're remarkably lucky to find these women who obviously love you. Or maybe it's not luck."

She lifted her head and met his eyes. She saw in them what she'd seen the first time he looked at her. Intensity, desire—that was there, too—and need. It was probably the need that got to her. The need that cried out and practically begged for the soft touch of someone who cared.

She leaned forward and kissed him. She felt the surprise in him, knowing he hadn't expected it. She ran her tongue over the seam of his mouth, loving the feel of him, loving the idea that she could do this again. The pain of missing him was gone and it felt as if she'd lost a hundred pounds. But when he opened his mouth, wanting to deepen the kiss, she pulled back.

As much as she wished it could be over, they weren't done yet. There was still one thing she had to know. It would hurt him, she thought. Hurt him to tell it, and so it hurt her to ask.

"Tell me why you went to jail, Dominic."

Chapter 12

"I need to know."

Dominic remained silent.

"They said you assaulted a man."

He closed his eyes and she could see his body tightening. There was no escaping the question. They'd gone too far now. It had to be everything between them or there could be nothing.

"I did."

"Why?"

"Because I hated him. And when I was eighteen, I wasn't as adept at controlling my emotions as I am now."

"Who was he?" Although she already suspected the answer, she thought the questions would help him get it out.

"My father," he exhaled.

Caroline, too, released the breath she'd been holding. "Tell me about him."

"What's to tell? He was a bastard. Worthless and mean-spirited. My mother was seventeen when they met. She was a migrant worker in the grape fields in Central California. I like to think it was his fault. That he seduced a girl who barely knew English, but she loved him."

"Sometimes you can't necessarily help it."

"That sounds like you're speaking from experience," he said.

Caroline wasn't going to lie. "I will admit there have been a few times in the past week where I wished I had just gotten a cat."

"Anyway, they married. How she managed to get him to do that, I'll never know, but it was legal. She became pregnant with me. Once that happened he left. She was devastated. But we had each other."

"She loved you." She remembered how defensive he'd gotten when she'd suggested that his mother abused him. There was devotion on his part. Had there been on hers as well?

"She did," he agreed. "But maybe only because I was a part of him."

Caroline said nothing. She simply processed the blow to her chest. She'd called him cold. Heartless. But he wasn't. Not really. He was just a man who had been abandoned by his father and made to believe his mother only cared for him because he reminded her of the man she loved.

It was a wonder that there was any softness in him at all. And it made her question whether or not he would ever be able to return the love she wanted to give him. She couldn't think about that. She needed the story. All of it. Then they had to figure out what the next step was going to be.

When this was over, she could decide if there was hope.

"She got sick," he continued. "Breast cancer, but she let

it go unchecked. By the time they diagnosed it, it had spread. We didn't have any money for doctors or hospitals, nowhere near enough for the type of care she needed. I was out of my mind with worry and guilt. Not her, though. She just seemed to accept it. Told me everything would be okay. I was seventeen, mostly raised, smart. She told me I had a chance to be something. But I wasn't ready to let go."

"No one ever is. Not when it's their mother."

"She was so young," Dominic insisted. "Too young to die. I worked three part-time jobs, but that just paid the rent and bought food. Medicine was out of the question. It was either go to him or rob a bank."

"He didn't help you."

"He told me he barely remembered her. I stood there looking at this man who was supposed to be my father, a man my mother was in love with when I was conceived, and he didn't even know who I was. The irony is I look like him. I have my mother's coloring, but his nose, his eyes, his chin. It sickened me, knowing I could look like someone I hated so much."

"Is that when it happened?"

"No. I left and went back home and held my mother's hand for the next few months while she died at home."

She wanted to reach out to him, but he stood and moved away from her. His arms crossed over his chest and the Do Not Touch sign was back up. "I'm so sorry."

"You would have liked her," he said over his shoulder. "She was sweet. Very relaxed about life in general. I knew it hurt her to lose him, but she carried that pain around with her like a badge of honor."

"That you could see that in her must mean you were very observant. I'm still trying to imagine the little boy. I bet you were serious."

"I was," he admitted sheepishly.

"I can imagine," she chuckled.

"Not like now," he corrected. "But I didn't let go, have fun as easily as the rest of the other boys. I suppose it's my nature. But the control, mastering my emotions, my anger, my rage, that all came from prison."

Her smile gone, she pressed. "Finish it."

"After she died I bounced around. I was in L.A. At some bar with a bunch of guys, boys really, but we thought we were bad. We hated the world and the world hated us. It was how I felt about life. I was boozed up and in more pain than I knew what to do with. Then he walked in. Total co-incidence. And really bad timing. I told him he killed her. I told him it was his fault. But really it wasn't. I should have worked harder to get her to see a doctor or found some way to get my hands on more money. I could have saved her."

"You couldn't have." This time, Caroline ignored the warning signs and stood to walk toward him. She didn't touch him, but she left little space between their bodies. "At least let that go. After all these years, please know that you couldn't have stopped what was happening to her body. Not without her help. It sounds like she didn't want to fight."

"She didn't," Dominic said. "But why? Why not at least try to live? For me."

"I can't answer that. Neither can you. But you're walking around with twenty-year-old guilt. It must be heavy. Let it go."

He ran his hands over his face and inhaled. "I picked the fight. We took it outside and I whaled into him with every ounce of strength I had in my fists. I spilled my anger all over him until the cops showed up and dragged me off his unconscious body." He paused and took a step away from her. "You need to know that, Caroline. What's living inside of me. I didn't even know I was capable of it until then. I had never felt that kind of rage before. But that night I couldn't stop it. I couldn't see past it. I was out of control."

"You were also drinking."

Dominic shook off her excuse. "That was the least of my problems. If anything it helped. Being drunk, I couldn't see clearly enough to land all of my punches. It was probably the only thing that saved his life, and mine for that matter."

"What happened to him?"

"I don't know. I guess they took him to a hospital. They took me to jail. Then a lawyer came in to tell me that the man I had attacked was pressing charges. I explained that he was my father, but that didn't seem to matter. Turns out it's not exactly legal to beat up your biological father. They gave me a public defender and the next thing I remember was the judge's gavel hitting the table sentencing me to eighteen months."

Tears welled in her eyes. He'd been a boy. An angry boy who had lost his mother. She wanted to rail at the injustice. She wanted to find his father and hurt him again. But that was done and if there was one thing she was certain of in life, it was that you had to look forward. It had taken her a long time to get there after her parents had died, but she was finally making steps.

"That's it, then. So what happens next?"

Dominic looked at her. "Next?"

"Next. You told me why you left. You told me why you went to jail. You told me you didn't kill Denny and I believe you. That means that someone else did. I'm guessing you have your theories. For that matter, I have some, too. Lucky for you, you married a mystery writer."

"This isn't a story in one of your books."

"I'm not suggesting it is. Nor do I want to play the role

of amateur detective. The first thing we need to do when we get back to San Jose is call the police."

"No," he said sharply.

"Dominic what choice do you have? You're innocent. I know it. Your sister knows it. They'll find out who did this and in the meantime you'll…"

"I'll be in jail," he growled. "I don't think you understood what I was trying to tell you before. I can't go back."

"But it's temporary," she reasoned.

"This isn't a question of not wanting to," he tried to tell her. "I. Can't. Go. Back."

"So that's it?" she asked, frustrated. "We forget all of this and leave. A life on the run. You and me on a beach in Mexico living under an assumed name."

He didn't answer. As the seconds ticked by and his grim expression didn't change, she finally understood. For as much as he'd hurt her already, it was still a surprise each time. Like he'd just kicked her out of bed again. The disappointment she felt was numbing and she was transported back to last night standing on her doorstep, weary to the bone with no hope for a happy ending. "You never had any intention of taking me with you."

"I needed to get you out of California. I needed you to be safe."

"Why?" she pushed. "Why did you care?"

If it was possible his eyes darkened even further. "You need me to answer that?"

Caroline thought about it. "Yes. I do. A few minutes ago you said you would follow me to the ends of the earth, but now you're disappearing again. You're always leaving me, pushing me away. Somehow. Do you really care about me?"

He moved but she stepped back out of his reach. "Caroline."

"What?" she barked even as she took more paces back. "You want me to believe something else? Then tell me."

Frustrated, he ran a hand through his hair. "Look, I'm not leaving to go to Mexico. I need to go back to California. I need to find out who did this. I need to know if Denny's program is out there somewhere. I told you in the wrong hands it could be dangerous."

She had to force herself not to roll her eyes. "Don't give me the dangerous software program bull. Fine. If you don't want to go to the police, then—"

"I *can't* go!" He shouted so loudly he startled her. It wasn't the first time he'd raised his voice, but this was different. She could see the veins standing out along his neck. Suddenly the image of him standing over his father and beating him senseless wasn't so hard to imagine.

It was as if she flipped some switch in him. The control he exercised over every gesture was gone. His arms spread out and then his fist slammed into his bare chest.

"This isn't some game with me. Prison took everything out of me, can you understand that? No, you can't! You were shut up here in your little ivory tower writing your stories having control over your characters' actions and emotions. I had no control. None!"

His breathing was ragged and Caroline found herself torn between the desire to go to him or run away.

"Every minute of every day was out of my control. Every second spent watching my back, my front. I used every instinct that I had ever been born with to survive. Everyone was the enemy inside. For seventeen months and twenty days, I was nothing. I couldn't pick and choose the feelings I wanted to keep in there. I couldn't stop the fear and the madness but keep everything else. All of it had to go. All of it. You said I was cold. You're right. So I'm not going to the police. And I'm not going back to prison. But I have to find out what happened to Denny. I have no choice."

"Then let me go with you," she said quietly.

Her soft whisper took him off guard and immediately he checked himself. He'd shouted at her again. She'd done nothing but want an answer and he'd screamed at her like a man out of control.

"I'm sorry I yelled."

"I don't want your apology. I want to go with you. I want to help you do whatever it is you need to do."

"I just got you out of there. You think I'm going to let you go back?"

Dominic let his head drop forward. Didn't she understand? Didn't she get that all of this was made worse by knowing what he put her through? He had taken her away from her sanctuary, had dragged her across the country on the promise of a family. It wasn't until he began to fear what she made him feel that he knew he was never going to be able to give her what she wanted.

She got too close. She pushed too hard. The night Denny died, he sat at his office desk and calculated exactly how long it would take to divorce her. To make her leave so he wouldn't have to hear her say at some unknown point in the future that she didn't love him anymore.

Then he'd left her in the presence of a killer. He had no choice but still it slashed a new wound in him. Did the murderer go to the house? Did the two of them communicate? The questions had driven Dominic crazy as he waited.

But that was all over. She was here. Safe. She believed him. Maybe she would stop loving him. Maybe she would even learn to hate him, but he couldn't risk her getting hurt. No matter how hard it was to leave her. He would.

Caroline spun on her heel and started down the stairs.

"Where are you going?" he questioned as he followed her.

"I'm going to let Munch out in the backyard. And then I'm going to call the airlines and book a ticket."

Shit.

"Caroline!" She was in the kitchen when he caught up to her. A grateful Munch was quickly doing her business in the small patch of grass beyond the sliding glass door.

Caroline reached for the portable that hung on the wall, but he stopped her, holding her hand against the receiver. "You cancelled the service."

"I'll use my cell."

"You won't. I won't allow it," he said between gritted teeth. She was really starting to piss him off.

"Last time I checked, I was a grown woman," she hissed back at him. "And the very last time I checked, our marriage wasn't legal, so even if you thought you had some control over me in that department, you're wrong."

He squeezed the hand under his, not hard, but enough to make his frustration known. "Can't you accept that I want to keep you safe?"

"I can. Can you accept that I want to go to California to help you resolve this? That I care about you, as difficult as you're making that right now, and that I don't want to see you hurt, either."

He paused trying to find some other answer, but there was none. "Do I have a choice?"

"Not really. If you leave, I'll just follow you." She jerked her hand out his grasp.

"You're stubborn," he accused her.

She nodded. "I was sort of keeping that under wraps until you got to know me better. My gut says we stay together. I figure since I've been doing nothing but listening to it for weeks now, I might as well keep on going."

"Look where that got you," he said humorlessly.

"I'm going with you."

"I don't want to hurt you," he said knowing that he probably wasn't done doing it.

"Another thing we agree on. I don't want you to hurt me, either."

Chapter 13

"What about Anne?"

They were cruising on an endless highway that Caroline was certain stretched across the universe. Dominic had decided driving was safer than booking a flight in case the police were monitoring airline travel. Plus the three or four days it would take them to get back to California would give them time to think and plan. Caroline's BMW had still been in her garage. Jump-starting the battery was all it took for them to be on their way.

Of course Munch had to be left behind at a neighbor of Caroline's. The dog obviously hadn't been happy, but at least there she was guaranteed steady meals and two young boys who were over the moon to be babysitting a dog. Still, she couldn't help but sympathize. She knew exactly how Munch felt.

Dominic didn't respond to her question, but a shrug of his shoulder said he didn't plan to explain himself again.

"Why are you so certain it's Steven?"

Steven had been Dominic's prime suspect from the get-go. She knew his reasons. As the last partner standing he had a lot to gain, he was the only other person besides Serena who had access to the financial records, and he'd been under pressure from his father-in-law to make good on the loan he'd been given. Maybe he felt that with Denny's new product, the whole pie was better than a piece.

"Why are you fighting the idea that it could be him?"

"Because I like him," she answered truthfully. "I would rather it be Anne or Russell. Or someone else entirely. A surprise character at the last second. An old enemy of Denny's from prison. A homicidal maniac who the police have already arrested."

"It doesn't work like that in your books," Dominic said. "There is always a reason. Murder like this, the setup, it isn't easy. It's thoughtful. Someone has to have a lot to gain to take the risk."

"How do you know how it works in my books?" Caroline cast a glance at him. His eyes remained fixed on the road but she thought she noted a faint flush in his cheeks. "You read one of them, didn't you?"

"You had a lot of copies on your shelves. It was a way to pass the time."

"I'm flattered," she said dryly.

He gave her a quick glance. "It was good. But it was obvious who the killer was. In the book I read, there was only one bad person among the cast. He had to be the murderer."

"I think that's why I can't imagine it's Steven. He doesn't seem like a bad person. He seems in over his head sometimes, like he's struggling to catch up with every-thing—his wife, his father-in-law, you. But I never sensed that he was evil."

"And you want to think it's Anne because you don't like her."

Maybe. Which wasn't necessarily fair. "She told me what happened between you two."

Silence for a beat. Then he asked, "Did she?"

"You seem surprised."

"It's not something I imagine comes up in polite conversation."

"I knew I was right about you two even if you didn't want to talk about it. I confronted her. She admitted that she made a pass at you. Said since it happened she's been trying too hard to be your friend, hoping that you would forget."

"I forgot the minute it was over."

Caroline wondered if Anne would be happy to know that. She didn't think so. It wasn't very flattering. But if this was a revenge plot for a spurned advance, why kill Denny? He was an innocent bystander.

"Tell me about the project Denny was working on. You said it was scary. Dangerous. What's so dangerous about a software program?"

Watching his profile, she saw him wince, as if being reminded of Denny's program made him nervous all over again.

"We're a software company that encrypts data. I told you what that means."

On the first night she met him. "You lock the data, send it over the Internet and then someone opens it with a key."

"Yes. Well, Denny wrote a program that acted as a skeleton key. He could open any lock."

"I don't understand."

"We have competitors," Dominic said. "Other software vendors who write the same kind of programs we do to encrypt data. We were starting to build a reputation in the industry as being more reliable because our competitors' software was being cracked. People were able to intercept the data over the Internet and decrypt it. And the stories were making news, causing an uproar because businesses are nuts about Internet security. With good reason. Financial transactions are just the tip of the iceberg of what's out there. Social Security numbers, private medical information."

Then it clicked. A skeleton key. "It was Denny wasn't it? He was doing it."

Dominic's fingers tightened over the steering wheel until his knuckles were white. "Yes. In an effort to make our software impenetrable he stumbled upon this program. He targeted a few major corporations. Two back east. One in L.A. Companies that pass personal information on their employees to insurance carriers. He was able to crack their network security and intercept the files. Then he unlocked the data and made it public. He promised me he didn't do anything with what he found. Just let it be known to both parties who were transmitting the data to one another what happened. The story got leaked to some local press. Anonymous hacker steals Social Security numbers. Was it front page news? No. But imagine you're a congressman sitting on a committee deciding which company you're going to trust to encrypt data for the government."

"Looks bad," Caroline admitted.

"Bad for them. Good for us. I couldn't believe it when he told me. I was furious. If it came out, our reputation would be destroyed. He'd be arrested. Not to mention what it would mean if people discovered there was a program that could make any protected data available to anyone who wanted it. It wouldn't be long before the criminal element descended."

"Why did he do it? Did this contract mean that much to you financially?"

Dominic paused obviously rolling the question around in his head. "Yes and no. We were doing okay. Taking jobs away from some of the bigger names in the industry. But this would have solidified us. It would have vaulted us from successful to the big time. But Denny doing anything for money doesn't make sense. He didn't care about the money. All he cared about was the work. The mental challenge of making something that nobody could beat."

"Pride. He wanted to show off that he was better than anyone else at what he did."

"Could be. But showing off usually entails two people. The person doing the showing and the person watching. I don't think Denny had any intention of telling me what he did. It wasn't until I pressed him that he caved first about the program, then about what he'd done."

Caroline thought of another problem. "Where is it?"

"The program?" Dominic grimaced. "I don't know. I know he wouldn't have put it out there on the company network. He never went anywhere without his laptop. That had to be in the car with him, so I imagine it was destroyed in the fire."

"Then the program is gone," Caroline concluded.

"One copy of it, yes. Denny would have had a backup."

"You're going to look for it, aren't you? That's the other reason we're going back."

"Yes. I have to believe that his death and that software program are related. I need to know not just who killed him, but if he got his hands on that damn program."

"Can I ask you if you're more worried about somebody using it unlawfully or that someone might expose what Denny did?"

He rubbed his eyes quickly and then focused on the road. He didn't say anything for a long time. "I wish I could tell you I'm some kind of hero and I want to do this to protect people's private information. I can't. That company is my life. It's everything I've ever made of myself. I can't watch it crumble. I won't. I'll find the program and destroy it along with any evidence of what Denny did. Then I'll find Denny's killer."

Caroline wanted to ask what he would do once he found him but she didn't.

"It's getting late," he said abruptly and pointed to an exit up ahead on the highway. "We'll pull over for the night."

The exit marked Radlytown consisted of a gas station, a fast-food restaurant and a one-floor motel that looked barely habitable. Dominic left Caroline in the car while he went to check in. He came back with a key and pulled the car around to the back of the motel so it couldn't be seen from the single road that split the town. It seemed like an unnecessary precaution in such an isolated place, but he apparently wasn't taking any chances.

They got out and Caroline stretched her legs and back, thinking a hot bath might help ease her tight muscles. When Dominic opened the door to their room, she immediately decided a bath was out of the question.

In a room that looked like this, even a shower might not be a good idea. Heck, she was pretty sure she would be better off using the ladies' room at the fast-food restaurant.

"I'm sorry," Dominic apologized, setting their bags inside by the door as he took in the accommodations.

"It's all right." Caroline pulled down the spread on the king-sized bed and examined the sheets. They were clean and smelled of strong laundry detergent. "It will do. But I am hungry."

"I'm sure the convenience store has some microwave burritos. Or if you are looking for something a little more upscale, there's a burger and fries."

A chuckle bubbled up and out of her mouth. It was a joke. He'd made a joke and while it was a lame one, she still had a hard time stopping herself from hiccupping with laughter. Probably since it had been so long since she could laugh about anything.

"I'll take upscale. I do have my standards."

Dominic smiled. For a second she thought he wanted to say something, but he shook his head. "I'll be back with the burgers and fries."

"I am going to pray the shower head spurts out clean hot water."

Dominic returned to the room with two bags of greasy food. He set them down on the single table in the room and stared at the bathroom door. The sound of running water told him she must have come to terms with the shower. He hoped for her sake it wasn't too grubby. He didn't like the mental image of her showering amongst the dirt. She was too good for that.

Too good for that, too good to be on the run with him. Too good for any of this. With a sigh, he sat down on the edge of the bed and for the tenth time wondered why he'd let her come with him.

Then he wondered what it would have been like to make this trip alone without her. Talking to him, pushing him to think, the whole time reminding him that he was in this with someone. A partner.

Dominic thought of Denny and how that partnership had ended. A swell of regret washed over him. It had been such a stupid trick of fate that had landed them together on the inside. Dominic had focused on maintaining his isolation. He hadn't talked to anyone, no one had talked to him. Anybody who'd tried to give him trouble he'd been strong enough to beat off.

Not Denny. Denny had been a wounded zebra at a lions' watering hole and the predators had known it. Bad timing had Dominic walking into a laundry room where Denny had been cornered by three thugs looking to do what predators did with the weak. There had been that moment, that split second where he had to decide whether to walk away and pretend he didn't see anything or fight for someone he didn't even know.

Dominic wondered if he would ever tell Caroline how close he'd been to walking out and what kind of person that made him. But in the end he hadn't. He'd stayed and fought and got the shit beaten out of him. Before anything else could happen, the guards found them and pulled everyone apart.

They'd been forced to spend two days in solitary, but as soon as Denny got out he'd tracked down Dominic and had pledged his everlasting loyalty. And he'd given it. Right up until the end.

"Who else did you tell about the program, Denny?"

The sound of running water was his only answer.

Turning toward the door, he thought about Caroline standing underneath a spray of hot water. His wife. He'd never believed he would have been the type to be so territorial, but one of the hardest things about being away from her was knowing she was out of his reach. Knowing, too, that at some point someone would have told her the truth about his name and his past, essentially forfeiting their marriage.

That thin tie, the connection that kept her linked to him, snapped with a few words, making it okay for her to leave him. But she hadn't. She'd stayed there in his house waiting. While he'd been waiting in hers. So desperate for any connection to her that he'd read one of her books searching for her in between the pages.

He looked down at his lap and saw that he was hard. Just the idea that she was so close, naked and wet had been enough to set him off. He wondered what she would think if he opened the door to the bathroom, pulled aside the curtain and joined her there.

He could lift her around his body, sink her down on his erection, let the hot water pound against her skin, while his hot flesh pounded up inside of her. A low growl escaped his throat as his body tightened with anticipation.

It was always this way with her. She brought out something feral in him, something he thought he'd left buried in his cell the day he was released. His life was about control now. Over his work, over everything—his decisions, his plans, his designs.

But with Denny's death, all that was gone, wasn't it?

He'd started to fight her because she took things out of his hands. Like his desire and his emotions. He would have, in fact, divorced her because of it. But what was the point of fighting her anymore?

The control he thought he had over his life was an illusion. One he'd held on to for so many years. But illusions eventually winked out of existence and all you were left with was the truth.

And the truth was there was little he could control.

He wanted his wife and he didn't care if he wanted her too much. He was tired of running, tired of worrying about what would happen if he let her get too close. He tossed off his shirt and toed out of his sneakers. When his hands reached for the buttons on his jeans, he saw that they shook.

Immediately, he stopped and took a deep calming breath.

He wouldn't take her against her will, and he wasn't sure what her will would be, so he needed to get a grip. Shucking off his pants he made his way to the bathroom door. He opened it and the steam and heat surrounded him. He saw her silhouette behind the thin opaque shower curtain. She was still, her hands no longer moving the washcloth over her body.

He pulled the curtain aside and their eyes met. His body couldn't hide its intent from her. There was uncertainty in her eyes and it cut him like a knife, but he moved forward. The spray of water hit his skin but he ignored it, instead focusing on her. Her body was wet and lush. It trembled slightly. He reached for her and brought her up against him. His sex pressed into her belly. Her breasts pushed against his chest. Her hands rested on his shoulders. He knew she still wasn't sure yet if she was going to use them to push him away or hold him.

Please hold me. Please.

"Caroline," he muttered dipping his head to take her lips, but she pulled away. Not her body. That was locked against him, his arm wrapped around her waist like a vise. Her eyes locked onto his and she seemed to be asking a question he didn't know the answer to.

Again he lowered his head, using his free hand to cup her face and hold her in place for his kiss. His lips took hers with a ferocity he could barely contain, and silently he pleaded with her to allow this moment. His tongue plunged against her closed mouth and when she gasped for air, he invaded her. Her heat, her taste, were all his to take.

But he didn't want to take so much as he wanted her to give.

He lifted his head and whispered her name again, barely heard over the sound of the water falling on their bodies.

"Let me," he whispered.

Slowly, her eyes on his the entire time, as if she wanted him to understand what she was offering, she slid her leg up against the outside of his until it was wrapped around his thigh.

She was completely open to him. "Caroline," he groaned with raw need.

With strong but unsteady hands, he lifted and turned her, pushing her back against the tiled wall of the shower. In one long firm motion he thrust his sex deep inside her. He could feel her shock, but she was slick and ready despite his lack of foreplay. He stilled his body until he felt her soften and succumb. Her legs wrapped around his waist and squeezed. Her heels bumped against his ass. For a second she squirmed against him as if she were trying to find some respite from the thick shaft that impaled her. But he gave her none and instead started to thrust hard.

"This is how I want you," he growled into her ear. "Nothing held back. Are you ready for this?"

He wouldn't withdraw, wouldn't leave her, but instead would only make his body go deeper and higher.

"Tell me," he urged.

Was she ready for this? No, she probably wasn't, but she wouldn't stop him. He was giving something to her. Instinctively, she knew that. Testing her in some way, too, to see if she could handle every element of who he was as a man.

She threw her head back against the shower wall and braced her hands against his shoulders. Her body was pinned by his. All she could do was feel. Every sense that she had was focused on the point of their connection. Heat radiated out from her center and began to make its way through her body at lightning speed. It was almost a difficult sensation—to feel so overwhelmingly aroused so suddenly.

He began to drive into her, this time pulling away a little more so he could push deeper. She felt branded. Stretched beyond her limits. She didn't know how it was possible to want him to stop yet equally powerful to want him to continue.

His hands gripped her butt and his fingers kneaded deep into her flesh. But the ache only added to her pleasure. Her body writhed against the slick wall at her back and she could hear herself crying and moaning.

He changed the tempo of his motion and slowed slightly so he could withdraw almost completely before thrusting back inside her. She screamed each time he did and the hands that clung to his shoulders she now used to dig into his muscles.

"More. Faster," she screamed.

"No. My way." He pulled out, letting the rounded head of his cock rest barely inside her passage, then flexed the muscles in his ass sending his shaft ripping through her.

"Ahhhh," she screamed again. Tears ran down her face, unnoticed against the streams of water that washed over them. Never before had she been so aware of her body. Its physicality. Never before had she felt each nerve, every muscle, the beat of her heart. She was being taken ruthlessly against a shower wall and her body sang in a delicious joyous celebration.

She was his, completely and utterly his.

And he was hers, completely and utterly hers. She wondered if he knew that.

Instinctively she tightened her inner muscles, grasping at his sex each time he tried to leave. She heard him groan, which only made her body clench harder.

"Don't," he growled, his face a picture of tortured pleasure.

"Then faster," she bargained. She felt the smile on her

face and had the devilish thought that she wished she could see this, see what he was doing to her. Watch his hips flex and know what it felt like on the inside.

Instead, she looked at him and saw the power of his need. His lips were tight, his cheeks flushed. His eyes...so hard. It should have frightened her, but it didn't. She would never be afraid of him. She would never be afraid of this. He was out of control, out of his mind with wanting her, but he would never hurt her.

His hands moved up and over her buttocks wrapping around her back, bring her into total contact with his body. He spread his legs to gain more balance against the wet bottom of the tub and leaned against her, pressing her more completely against the wall.

Their eyes were centimeters apart. Their mouths were open, their breath mingled.

"Don't close your eyes," he ordered her.

"I won't," she gasped as she felt him begin to move again, this time more quickly.

It was hard to obey, but watching him was intense. She saw so much of who he was, his vulnerability and his pain mixed with his strength and fortitude.

And so they both kept their eyes open while he rode her hard and fast, snapping his hips and pushing her beyond mere pleasure. Then something inside her exploded and she was overcome with a wave of heat so intense she feared she might melt from within. It shook her to her very core. Then her body opened in a deep yawning stretch that sent pleasure coursing first through her womb, then her limbs.

She heard him shout, felt the pulse of his orgasm filling her deep inside, then his body was crushing her against the tile, his strength and his ability to hold her upright seemingly gone.

"I love you," she whispered against his shoulder as her head dropped forward. "There are times I don't want to, but I can't stop."

She felt him jerk, but he said nothing. He reached out and turned off the water, then carefully lifted her against his body and took them both out of the shower and to the bed.

She was draped across his body, her head resting on his heart, feeling it beat beneath her ear. A soft sound stirred her and she lifted her head so that she could hear it better.

"Please don't stop. I don't want you to stop."

Chapter 14

Nora pulled her rental car off the road along the winding route that led up the hillside to Dominic's residence. Lucky for her, a neighbor farther down the road was having a party, and the street was lined with cars. Hers would not stand out. She got out of the car and stared up at the hill.

There was still some distance between her and Dominic's house and it wouldn't be an easy hike, but she couldn't risk getting any closer. She knew that patrol cars still passed the house a few times a night, and she didn't want to do anything that would alert them.

Rather than stick to the road, she headed into the under-growth, which would provide cover, and made her way through the trees and bushes. The climb wasn't so steep that she couldn't handle it, but by the time she reached his house she was winded.

Taking a minute to catch her breath, she decided that it

had been too long since she'd been to the gym. She was starting to become one of those out-of-shape computer nerds whose only exercise was manipulating a mouse.

"As soon as I get back," she promised herself. Her breath restored she made her way to the enclosed pool.

She studied the sliding glass door that led from the patio into the pool area. The catch lock was simple and easily handled. No doubt the house was wired for security, which meant she was only going to have a few seconds to get inside and deactivate it. She reached for the small tool kit she'd tucked away in the fanny pack attached to her waist. She slid a slim flat-end screwdriver in between where the door met the glass wall and flicked up the latch.

As soon as she did she could hear the alarm inside begin its insistent chirping counting down the time she had to turn it off.

Moving quickly she circled the pool, slid another glass door aside, this one luckily unlocked, and entered Dominic's study. The alarm box was on the wall behind his desk. Instantly she removed the plastic covering that protected the system, and went to work on it with a small pair of wire cutters. She sliced first one and then a second connecting wire, which killed the battery and cut off the signal to trigger the alarm.

The alarm stopped mid chirp.

"Like taking candy from a baby," Nora muttered and made another mental note to tell Dominic that he needed to upgrade his security system.

Besides the kit, she removed a small flashlight from her belt and twisted it until a thin beam blinked on. She flicked it around the room, but quickly realized that the moonlight shining through the glass gave her more than enough light to work by. Dominic's desk was empty except for the monitor.

Mark had unexpectedly dropped by her hotel that morning. She'd been hoping for news on Dominic. The fact that he was still in hiding worried her. If he got it into his head to run, then there would be no coming back from that. As long as Caroline had stayed, she had hope that he would return for her. She didn't care how long they had known each other. If Dominic married her, then he planned to stay committed to her. For life. It was the nature of the beast.

But Caroline had bolted and there was still no word from Dominic. And Mark's report had only been to say they had found nothing on Dominic's home or office computers—which, of course, they wouldn't because what she hid, she hid very well—and had returned both of them to his place.

Only they weren't here.

Thinking maybe the cops had left them upstairs, Nora headed for the steps leading up to the next level of the house. When she didn't instantly see anything, she cursed.

A soft noise followed her curse and instantly she froze. Lifting her head slowly she spotted a dark form moving toward her from the foyer.

"Dominic?" she whispered hopefully.

No answer.

As she went back to reach for her weapon, the figure charged. Instantly she felt an arm wrap around her waist dragging to her to the ground. Reacting quickly, she wedged a knee between her attacker's legs and drove it up fast and high.

She heard a woof of air, a groan and then suddenly the person was rolling off her and with very good reason. She'd correctly identified the mystery figure as a man. Moving quickly, she straddled his chest and pushed her knees solidly against two biceps, pinning his arms to the ground.

"Who are you?" she asked as she reached behind her back for her weapon.

"Agent Shortcake, I'm offended. You don't recognize my moves?"

"Goddamn it, Hernandez," Nora cursed. His features were just visible in the dark, but his smile and the flash of white teeth were unmistakable.

"You know I've had fantasies about us in this position, but in them you were wearing a lot less clothes."

Disgusted, Nora crawled off his body and stood up. "What the hell are you doing here?"

He regained his feet and laughed. "That's a joke, right?"

Then she understood what had happened. The police wouldn't have returned Dominic's computers even if they hadn't found a damn thing on them. Stupid. Stupid. If she hadn't been so fixated on what she needed to do, she would have realized that.

"This was a setup. You told me the police returned his property to the house because you knew I would come here."

He shook his right leg a few times as if making sure all his parts still worked. "First things first. I let you win that fight on purpose."

"In your dreams," she muttered.

"Second, you can't pick up a tail to save your life. I was, like, half an inch off of your bumper the whole way up here."

"I was distracted," she said. Annoyed with herself, she made her way back to the living room and sat down on the couch. She figured he was going to want some answers and there was no point in not being comfortable.

Mark hit a few of the switches on the wall panel and watched the house light up. He made his way into the living room, stopping to admire the view of the ocean in the distance. "Man, I would love to have a place like this."

"It's a nice house. Are you going to tell me why you set me up?"

He turned back to her, his normally easy smile gone. He was all business.

"Are you going to tell me why you fell for it?"

Because she was a chump, Nora thought. The truth was, she wasn't really all that experienced as a field agent. It wasn't as if solving murders and breaking into houses and wrestling with cops was her terrain. She spent her days at the Bureau behind a wide-screen monitor.

Still, giving herself a little pat on the back, she'd handled two out of three okay.

"I have a buddy in the Justice Department," Mark began. "I called him a few days ago. He called his buddy over at FBI and confirmed that you worked there in the lab as a computer geek—"

"Lady," she insisted.

"Computer lady," Mark repeated. He sat next to her on the couch, the two of them staring straight ahead toward the windowed wall. "You're not a field agent and probably the last person the FBI would send even if they would have sent anyone. Which I pretty much figured from the very first. My instincts are gold. Anyway, I called, got the switchboard, asked for you and was informed that you were on vacation for the next two weeks and was there any-one else that could help me. I considered asking for your boss. Thought maybe he could tell me why you went rogue, but I decided to ask you instead."

"So now you know."

"I don't know shit. I know you don't want this guy to be guilty. Who is he? Your lover? And please say no."

"No." She laughed harshly.

"Ex-lover, then."

"No."

Mark scowled. "Am I going to have to get rough with you again?"

"I think we both know I'm not exactly afraid of you."

"Spill it, shortcake. Or I make that call to your boss. I can't imagine that the Federal Bureau looks kindly on this sort of behavior."

"Dominic Santos—" Nora began.

"Butler," Mark corrected her. "Don't forget."

"Not likely. Dominic is my brother."

Mark blew out the air in his lungs in a slow woosh. "Why do I feel like I just stepped into the middle of a bad soap opera?"

"Dick Butler was my father. He abandoned my mother and me much in the same way he did Dominic and his mother. My mom remarried and my stepfather adopted me."

"Why didn't you just… Oh, I get it. You know about the fake identity. Knowledge of criminal activity."

Nora nodded tightly. "Exactly. Of course I would never report him, but if my superiors found out I knew about it, I don't know what would happen. Dominic made me promise never to tell anyone about our relationship. We knew. That's all that mattered."

"What did you think you were going to find on the computer?"

"An e-mail that he sent to me the night of Denny's death. He told me about this software program that Denny had created, what it could do, what it could mean. He thought the government was going to have to get involved and he was right. When I bypassed his security that first day in the office, I transferred the e-mail to a file where it wouldn't easily be found so I could have a few days to discover what was going on. I knew he hadn't killed Denny. But he's been gone too long and I'm afraid he might run permanently. I've got to prove his innocence now and find a way to get him to come home."

"So you were here to put the e-mail back in his box. Then what?"

"I was going to tell your guys to check the computer again. Of course I have the e-mail on my computer back in D.C., but this seemed more expedient."

"Either way, you're exposed."

"Getting fired is a small price to pay for my brother's life."

"You two are close, huh?"

"No. Not really. But Dominic saved my life. Not too long ago, I was a rebellious, smart-mouthed teenager with a chip on my shoulder because my real daddy didn't love me. Also I had a natural propensity for trouble."

Mark smiled. "Rebellious? Chip? You're kidding me, shortcake. That doesn't sound like you at all."

Nora bumped up against his shoulder good-naturedly, letting him know she didn't care for his sarcasm. "Let's just say my personality was a lot more magnified back then. I had a natural gift for computers and ended up tracking down Dominic. I threatened to expose him if he didn't give me money so I could run away. He gave me a job instead. I was actually Denny's assistant for a few years. This was long before Steven showed up. Dominic made sure I went to college and then when the FBI wanted to recruit me, we both decided it would best to keep our relationship to ourselves."

"The FBI would have done a background check."

"Dick Butler was dead by then. They never looked farther than that. They spoke with Dominic, but as my employer, not my brother."

"So you knew Denny."

"Yeah," she admitted sadly. "He was a sweet guy. Harmless. His head was always in whatever program he was working on. I was convinced he wouldn't have remembered to eat unless I reminded him. I can't imagine who would have wanted to kill him."

"What's this program?"

Nora opened her mouth to explain, but Mark interrupted her with a raised hand.

"And don't give me a bunch of computer mumbo jumbo and megawatts and RAM and all that crap. Just the basics."

"According to Dominic, Denny has a program that can unscramble anyone's encryption code. Can decrypt any data regardless of what software was used to encrypt it in the first place."

"I'm with you so far. And this is bad?"

"This is very bad," Nora answered. "Imagine having the power to unlock any and all secured data being transferred over the Internet. This kind of program, in the wrong hands, would be seriously dangerous."

"Okay. That makes things simple. Somebody killed Denny to get their hands on the program and whoever that was, he set up Santos to cover his tracks. So who would have known about the program?"

"That is a very good question. Unfortunately, the only person I think who can answer that is…"

"Dominic," Mark concluded.

"Dominic."

"Then I guess we better hope he wants to be found."

"He'll come back. I know it."

"You just said you're afraid he's gone rabbit for good."

"I'm panicking, that's all. He didn't run because he killed Denny. He ran because he needed time to figure out who did. Once he does, he'll come back. Until then, all we can do is help him put the pieces together."

Nora lifted her feet up on the coffee table and settled deeper into the leather couch. In a way it was a relief to finally be able to share her thoughts with someone. And Hernandez wasn't stupid. In fact, he was probably the best ally Dominic could have, even if he was somewhat unwilling.

"So now that you know he didn't do it, who do you think did?" Nora asked.

Mark gave her a doubtful look. "I don't know shit."

"I told you he sent an e-mail to me that night. It's going to confirm his alibi."

"Sweetheart, I already know you tampered with the computer to hide the e-mail. How do I know you didn't put it out there in the first place? That e-mail proves nothing."

She huffed in annoyance. "What's your theory, then? Dominic killed Denny and contacted me, an FBI agent, to come help him cover up his murderous and embezzling tracks by concocting some story about a big bad computer program?"

"You know, when you say it like that, it sounds a little far-fetched."

"Hernandez," she snarled.

"Shortcake," he returned ominously. "Drop it. I've still got an ex-con on the run, a bride that's flown the coop, one standing partner with a devoted but spoiled wife, a sleazy father-in-law and now a half sister who wants to believe her brother is innocent and isn't afraid to lie and tamper with evidence to make sure that happens."

Nora's shoulders slumped. "You know, when you say it like that…."

"Exactly."

"So what's next?"

"What's next is you are going to get your pretty little ass on a plane back to Washington and let me figure this out without your interference, which, by the way, is a criminal act."

"I'm not leaving," she said stubbornly.

"Fine. I'll call your boss and let him know that you like to break laws on your vacation." Mark stood up from the couch. "What do you think he'll have to say to that?"

"You wouldn't."

He just looked at her over his shoulder.

"You would," she said glumly. "I don't care. Go ahead and spill, I'm not leaving until I know who killed Denny and am sure Dominic has been cleared."

Mark sighed. He'd expected as much, but that didn't mean he wouldn't follow through with his threat. Not that he liked the idea of being a tattletale. As a cop, it wasn't in his nature to rat out one of his own. But he liked even less the idea of her doing something to screw up his case once he made it. As much as she tickled his fancy, he really couldn't let her continue to interfere. On the flipside of that argument, her reasoning had been pretty sound throughout the investigation. She hadn't been the worst partner he'd ever had.

"Out of curiosity only, who do you think it is? Steven Ford?"

"Could be," she answered quickly. "Could be someone we haven't even considered. Someone else who might have access to Dominic's computer."

"The secretary," Mark muttered.

"Who?"

"Serena. Remember Ford thought it was possible that she might know Dominic's password. He said he gave it to her occasionally, but then would change it. Maybe the last time he forgot."

"Guess that means we need to talk to Serena."

"Guess that means *I* need to talk to Serena. You're going home." Mark figured he had about a fifty-fifty shot of making that happen.

"Am not." She stood up and crossed her arms over her chest in defiance.

"Are too," he said before he could stop himself.

"Am not."

"Are too." Make that forty-sixty.

"Am not."

He snapped his mouth shut and struggled for patience. After all, he was not five years old. "Yes, you are."

"No, I'm not."

This, he decided, was going to be a long night.

Chapter 15

"What time is it?"

"Early," Dominic answered in a quiet whisper. "Go back to sleep."

"I can't. I keep thinking."

Thinking about leaving him? Loving him? He wanted to ask but he didn't want the answer. Forty-eight hours ago he'd been ready to walk out on her, tucked safely back in her tower where none of the ugliness of his past or present could touch her. Now he wanted to enfold her inside him so she would never not be a part of him.

He hated feeling this way. Hated how freaking vulnerable it left him, but he had no choice now. She'd cracked something open and he wasn't sure if he had the strength to close it.

Hated the feeling, yes, but he couldn't hate her. Not when she was nestled against his side, her hand over his heart, her lips every so often brushing a kiss against his puckered nipple.

"When do you think we'll make it back to Half Moon Bay?"

Not thinking about him at all, but about the situation instead. He wasn't sure if he was annoyed or not. "Two more days. Less if we drive straight through."

"I want this over."

Understatement of the year. He knew his reasons, but what were hers?

She loved him. She'd said it. Twice. But she also said there were times she didn't want to and he wondered how strong her will was. Could she force her feelings to change? Direct them to behave?

He hadn't been able to. That's why when he'd left her that night after they fought, he had been certain that he couldn't stay with her. He wouldn't be able to control his emotions as he'd hoped. It couldn't be halfway. Not with her. He'd plan to cut her out. Eject her from every pore of his body. It was the only way.

Just as he'd done in prison. All feelings, all emotions gone. It was how he survived. When he finally got out, it had been easier to keep going that way. To keep himself apart from everyone.

But then Nora showed up and made him laugh. Denny continued to need protecting. And Steven. Steven had felt like a friend. Little by little, year by year, they had made him ready, he realized. So that when he met Caroline the crack in his impenetrable defenses that had been forming and growing larger had just burst open. Busted so wide, so fast that it had scared the hell out of him and he'd wanted to close it off.

Not without good reason, either.

Denny was dead. Steven was most likely his killer and Dominic's enemy, and Caroline didn't want to love him. Plus he couldn't imagine how funny Nora would be when they met up again. He wondered if their secret had been revealed with his past's unveiling. Dominic could only speculate what kind of trouble that might cause her at work.

Shut it down. Seal it up. Close it off and don't think about anything. Life as a zombie. Dominic remembered what it felt like to live that way and was surprised at how much he didn't want to go back. Despite the pain that came with letting people in.

Caroline turned slightly and he could feel her shifting and sliding along his body. He felt his penis stiffen and adjusted his hips so she wouldn't bump his erection. There was no reason to advertise his arousal when he knew she couldn't possibly be interested again.

He'd been rough earlier. Too demanding for her slight body. She'd practically collapsed in his arms when it was over. He closed his eyes and recalled the feeling of coming inside her. It had rocked his body from his spine to his toes and back again. He thought their sex had been good before, but he hadn't been prepared for the rush of pleasure that hit him. He'd never before gotten off so much on the idea of filling someone up with himself.

"I didn't use a condom," he blurted.

"Hmm?"

Her lips moved and this time she kissed the spot just above his brown nipple. He wondered if she was going to suck on it and felt himself grow harder. Clamping down on his desire he said, "Before. I didn't use a condom."

She sat up and the sheet slid from her body. Instinctively his hand covered her exposed breast. "We haven't used one from the beginning."

He had to pull his hand away, let her softness go. As his fingers brushed her, he found her nipple was hard, too. "That was before when we were trying to start a family."

"You don't want that anymore," she said, her head low, her voice tight.

"You do?" he asked, stunned.

"I…"

He watched her open her mouth as she searched for words, but eventually she had no answer. He didn't blame her. "You don't have to say anything. I understand."

She stared at him, but in the darkened room he couldn't make out her expression.

"What do you think you understand?"

"I'm an ex-con, for one."

"I don't care about that," she replied instantly.

"You should," he said and thought he saw her body jerk. "Not that you need to worry about the unprotected sex. I know the stories about prison. Hell a lot of them are true. But nothing ever…I mean, that wasn't a problem for me. Mostly because of the reputation I established as a son of a bitch. I didn't do drugs, didn't use needles. Anyway, I was tested when I got out. For everything. Just because I had to know I was clean."

She rested a hand on his face. "I know you. You would never put me at risk."

"It goes beyond that, Caroline. My past won't be something I'll be able to hide anymore. It will affect my work, how people deal with me. It will permeate everything. It's why I worked so hard to leave it behind. That stain will follow me. You'll be married to an ex-con. Your child's father will be an ex-con. It never goes away."

"That stain is there only if you let it be. I don't see it."

He wished he suffered from her naïveté. "Caroline, I'm

not getting you pregnant. At least not now, with things so uncertain."

She rolled away from him and lay flat on her back, the sheet pulled up to her neck.

He'd upset her, but he also knew that his argument was sound. Getting her pregnant before all of this was resolved was not an option. Leaving a child while he went off to jail definitely was not going to happen. If they made it, if they could find a way, then maybe. But only when he was certain she understood what it meant to be with a man who had a past.

"Why did you pick me?" Caroline asked after a moment.

"I don't know what you mean."

"From the other applicants. Why did you pick me? And don't tell me it was because of my career being suited to being alone a lot. You weren't thinking about that when you started. Surely you were looking for a type."

A type, yes, absolutely. A robot like him. Beautiful, serene, unemotional, unintrusive. Unloving. Not Caroline. He hadn't been looking for her. "I was."

"Part of the package had to be a certain age range," she continued clearly heading toward some conclusion. "You told me you wanted children. In fact, I'm pretty sure your only motivation for going to the agency in the first place was because you wanted a child. Because of the deal you had with your partners. Tell me I'm wrong."

He wouldn't lie to her. Not at this point. "You're not. I wanted a child. Someone I could leave my company to."

"Okay, so I'm thirty-five. My biological clock is ticking. Why would you pick me?"

There was a tension in her voice that he didn't understand. "You're upset because I want to put off getting you pregnant until this over. We're not talking years, Caroline."

"I know." She touched him again, her hand closing over his arm. "I just feel like we're running out of time. For so many things. But that's not why I asked you why you picked me. You were a man trying to find someone to have a child with. You should have picked someone younger. I know that about you, Dominic. Your choice should have been rational. Logical. So why did you pick me?"

"Your smile." The answer sprung to his lips so quickly. It made him feel foolish. He smiled unconsciously, tucking his hands behind his head, looking at the ceiling. "Not much of a rational decision, is it?"

"No."

Since he'd opted for honesty, there was no point in stopping. "It was the first thing I saw in the picture they sent me. I thought that smile was for me. When you looked into the camera, I thought you were smiling straight at me. When you answered my first e-mail, I knew I wanted to meet you. I didn't care about your age or whether or not you could have children. When we spoke on the phone, I got hard. Rationality went out the window."

She moved again and this time her hand didn't touch his arm. Instead, it slid down his belly until she was holding the erection he'd been trying to hide from her. He closed his eyes and groaned, thinking of the condoms he didn't have.

"Caroline," he breathed, ready to reach for her hand to pull it away.

"You don't have to get me pregnant," she said as she kissed his chest, then dipped her tongue into his belly button. She lifted her head. "In fact, I'm pretty sure it will be impossible this way. But at least you'll get to feel my smile. Up close and personal."

And he did. First her smile. Then her tongue. Then her mouth. And then there was nothing but the pleasure.

* * *

"How much farther?" She felt his gaze on her and cringed. "Fun fact about me. I don't like long car rides. Even when I'm driving."

He chuckled softly. "Eight, ten more hours."

Caroline pushed down harder on the gas pedal. The landscape in front of her was barren and brown everywhere she looked. Endless and unchanging. It disturbed her because as hard as she stared, she couldn't see what was coming over the next small rise. Couldn't see anything but the space around her.

She needed to drive through it, get past it, so that she could see something else.

Like her future.

She thought about what she told him, how there were times she didn't want to love him, and then she wondered if she truly had any control over that. He hadn't returned the words, hadn't whispered a hint about what he felt for her. Instead, he told her he didn't want to get her pregnant. Always with him it was one step forward, then one step back.

But she knew he felt something for her. Something strong. It was in his voice when he talked about her picture. It was there when they touched.

A connection.

At least the sex made her feel less insane about turning her back on her life to follow an ex-con on his quest to expose a killer. That kind of connection didn't just happen between two people. It made the risk worth it. Of course, she wondered if Bonnie thought the same way about Clyde.

Caroline knew nothing had been resolved last night. The sex had been intense and amazing, but in the end it was just sex. There had to be more between them if their marriage was to succeed. But she could admit that she was more anxious than ever to get back to where this started and finish it.

"And the plan when we get there?"

"I've been thinking about it. I think I should try to contact Serena."

"You think she might be involved?"

"No. Not with Denny's death. But someone had to have access to my computer to manipulate the financial statements. She would have seen something. Maybe heard chatter among other people in the office. I don't know. Serena says little but she hears everything. If there is a chance Steven didn't have his hand in this, maybe she can help us. I can trust her." After a beat he added. "I think."

Very reassuring, but she bit her lip. She liked that there was a plan. They would contact Serena first and find out what she knew. Then try to find where Denny might have hidden his super-key program. Once they had the pieces in place, they could go to Nora and the police.

It could be over. It would be over.

And then Caroline was probably going to have to decide if she was ready to get married.

Again.

Chapter 16

"Damn it!" Mark cursed. "Not again. How could this happen twice?"

Mark and Nora stood in the middle of Denny's office and looked around for the tornado that had ripped through the place.

"You seem to be under the impression that yellow tape with the words *Crime Scene* on it is enough to keep a murderer out. You might want to rethink that idea."

"Don't mess with me, shortcake. I'm already pissed off."

Nora shut her mouth. The day hadn't been going well for them, but on the plus side he'd let her ride along with him. And he hadn't threatened to call her boss in the last hour. Well, once when she'd given him grief over stopping for a pack of cigarettes. He didn't call, though, and he didn't buy the cigarettes. Win-win.

On the downside, when they'd shown up at Serena's

apartment to ask her a few questions it was evident that she had packed up and cleared out. There wasn't a single personal item except for some secondhand furniture. The apartment manager had bitched about having to pay someone to haul away the couch, bed and dresser, but since Serena had left no forwarding address he was satisfied the security deposit would cover it.

Nora hadn't felt the need to point out that the secretary's disappearing act was awfully suspicious. Nor did she mention that a woman living as frugally as Serena seemed to would not forfeit a security deposit without a good reason.

Irritated by the secretary's absence, and probably just to annoy Nora, Mark offered up a theory that Serena could have run to protect Dominic. If Dominic contacted her and offered her enough money to get out of Dodge, there's no reason to think she wouldn't go. After all she'd been his loyal secretary for ten years.

Nora told Mark his theory was lame.

That hadn't helped his mood.

Their next stop was to check Denny's residence again, since this time they knew what they were looking for. The crime scene seal had been broken and every room in the spacious penthouse condo had been trashed. It was chaos on top of chaos.

Bookshelves overturned. Kitchen plates smashed on the tile floor. Every desk and dresser drawer open. Clothes strewn about. Files, notes on programming and CDs cracked in half and scattered on the floor.

In fact, his house looked a lot like his office currently did.

A smashed coffee mug, an overturned computer chair, text books, magazines and yellow legal pads littering every surface. Nora recalled that Denny wasn't the neatest guy, but this was a little extreme.

"My guess is that someone left this place in a little bit of snit when he didn't find what he was looking for," Mark concluded. "Just like the condo."

He reached down and picked up some of the stacks of pads and magazines.

"What gave it away for you? Because that plastic fork sticking out of the flat-screen monitor was my first clue." Nora put down the laptop she'd brought with her and picked up the overturned chair and set it back on its wheels.

"You ever give that wise mouth of yours a break?"

She sat on the chair and pushed off with her legs to roll herself closer to the workstation. "Only when I'm sleeping. Or kissing."

Immediately, his eyes were drawn to her mouth. Just like she knew they would be. "I hate you," he muttered.

"No, you don't. But let's put that aside for now. Obviously someone was in here. And as you deftly concluded, good money says that he didn't find it. No reason to destroy mugs and a monitor if you have what you're looking for."

"So get to it," he said.

"Get to what?" she asked staring at the mess. "You need to call your crime scene people and have them look for prints here once they're done with the condo."

"Prints aren't going to do me a lot of good if I can't find out who they belong to. I need the thing this person is after. Which means I need you to act geek and figure out where our boy might have hidden it."

As much as she wanted to be insulted, the truth was it wasn't that hard for her to think like Denny would have in this particular situation. She'd worked on enough programs, programs that she'd poured her creative heart and soul into, to know how important backing up everything was. And knowing Denny like she did, there was probably more than one duplicate file—one off-site, in case of catastrophe and the building caught fire, and one he could easily access to restore the program in case he botched up something and wanted to start over.

She opened a drawer attached to the workstation and found about thirty flash drives tangled inside. The drawer beneath it contained a stack of CDs. Some in cases, some loose. Others had been tossed on the floor. Stepped on.

That didn't make sense. Why hadn't the person looking for his work taken everything? If Denny was going to back something up, make a hard copy, it would have most likely been on a flash drive. Easier to carry, easier to hide. But a CD was still possible.

Destroying the disks didn't make sense unless the killer had already gone through each one as well as the flash drives and found nothing special on any of them. That's a lot of time spent at a marked crime scene. "You have gloves right?"

"Yeah. In the car."

"You should get them. Whoever was in here definitely would have handled the CDs and memory sticks. I don't want to mess up any prints. I have to assume these have all been checked, but I've no choice but to go through them again."

Mark picked up one of the sticks by the attached band that could be used to wear the device around a wrist. "Do you know what you're looking for?"

"Not really. I'll recognize Denny's style. How he used to think. I should be able to read any of his programs. If something strikes me as beyond the norm, I'll know."

Mark saw the opened drawers filled to the top and groaned. "This is going to take forever."

"That's probably what the person who trashed this room thought. But I've got something he didn't have."

"What's that?"

"Patience," she answered smugly.

Mark left and came back with a kit that had a couple of pairs of thin plastic gloves. He called in the crime scene to headquarters and let them know that when the team was done with the condo, they had a new location to process. As Nora began to feed each of the CDs into her disk drive, her frustration grew exponentially.

"Okay, forget it. There's no way I'm going to be able to go through all of these."

"What happened to patience?"

"Patience split twenty CDs and ten memory sticks ago."

"Just keep looking."

Nora was about to ask what he was doing in the meantime and saw that he was stacking the magazines and text books and reading whatever was on the legal pads apparently without much success. She could have told him it was a waste of time. Denny had his own language. There was no way he would have left anything decipherable on paper.

When one of the piles he'd created toppled over he cursed, but then reached for something on the floor. "That's interesting."

"What?" Nora asked as she popped out a CD and put a new one in.

"Glamour."

She glanced at the magazine in his hand. "Fifty ways to improve your sex life. That's on page 162, if you're interested."

"It's not the article," he sneered. Although he immediately started flipping pages. "It's the magazine that I'm interested in."

"Having a fall fashion crisis?"

Mark ignored her and pointed to the fallen magazines

scattered on the floor. "They're all computer geek magazines. What's a guy like Haskell doing with a chick magazine?"

"There's a half-naked woman on the cover. Maybe he was interested in the pictures."

"Trust me, if he was going to buy a magazine to look at pretty girls, there are better ones to choose from. No, this is a magazine for a woman. You think he had a girlfriend?"

"Doubtful. You had to know Denny. He wasn't into people. Just computers. If he was having any kind of sex, it was online."

"I'll make sure they're careful with this one when checking for prints. You find anything yet?"

"Nope."

Each attempt netted her more of the same. More files. More programs. As she scanned each one looking for something unique she felt Mark hovering over her shoulder. Then she heard him breathing.

"I have a new theory," she announced. "The person who stabbed the monitor had a partner who liked to lean over her shoulder and piss her off. Finally, she snapped. Only what you don't realize is that before she shoved the plastic fork into the monitor, she shoved it up her partner's…"

Hands raised in surrender he took several large steps back. "I get it, I get it," he said. "No pestering."

"Go kill some time. A man can always make use of fifty ways to improve his love life."

Dominic watched Caroline in the phone booth across the street for what felt like days although he knew it was only minutes. It had taken them almost an hour to find another pay phone that worked since he didn't want to risk a trace on his cell now that he was back in San Jose. The section of town they were in wasn't the best, but beyond the threat of junkies and muggers was the worry of a patrol car that might wonder what a BMW was doing in the neighborhood.

Rain that had picked up since they reached the city limits started to fall harder until his vision of Caroline was almost completely obscured. He was about to go after her, not taking the chance of even remotely letting her out his sight, when he saw her dash across the empty street toward him.

"She's not there," she said as soon as she closed the passenger door behind her. "Or she's not answering. Not on any of the numbers you gave me. And no answering service on the home phone, which seems odd."

Where the hell was Serena? He'd given Caroline her direct line at the office, the cell phone he'd provided for business needs and finally her home phone. They'd tried earlier this morning as soon as they reached the city limits, again around noon and now after the office was closed. "I wanted to know more before we took the next step."

"The next step meaning finding where Denny hid his program?" Caroline assumed.

Dominic nodded. "Our best chance is the office. Denny changed how he handled his backups. He got frustrated with the memory sticks because he was always losing them. Instead he set up a special mapped drive on the network that only he had access to. If I could get my hands on the network backup cartridge, it's likely that Nora would be able to find and access his drive."

Caroline reached out to grab his hand. She squeezed it and waited until he turned his hand and squeezed hers back. "This is it. Let's go."

He drove as carefully as a man who knew the entire police department was looking for him should. Eventually they made it to his office and he parked across the street from the lobby entrance.

"Wait here" he said automatically.

"No," she said clutching his arm before he could leave the car. "You can't go in. There will be security guards inside, not to mention cameras."

"I hired those guards."

"Then you know that you recruited quality people. People who wouldn't hesitate to call the police given what they think they know about you."

He sighed and shut the door. "There might be a way in through the garage."

"There's a way in through the front door. You just can't go through it. I can."

"Absolutely not."

"Why? I'm not a suspect. I can tell them that I returned to town and that I suddenly decided I want a picture of us that you left in your office."

The idea seemed ridiculous.

"I'll cry when I tell them," Caroline added. "Men never know what to do with a sobbing woman."

Great. He was turning his wife into a con artist. Unfortunately, she was right, and a few tears might work. "Okay. Let me draw you a map of where we keep the server. The backup cartridge that's in there will work." Dominic reached behind him for a brown fast-food bag that had been tossed in the backseat, and Caroline found a pen in the glove compartment.

He indicated the floor, showed her the elevators and stair wells, and directed her through two turns, then put an X over the room where the network server was stored. "You'll see a large black tower. It's the only computer in the room. There's a small blue button that will eject the cartridge. Get it and come back."

She nodded confidently and opened the passenger door. This time, he stopped her with a hand on her arm. He couldn't say everything he wanted to say, not here in a car right before she was about to break into his office on his behalf. Instead, he leaned forward and kissed her. "Be careful."

She nodded again and scurried across the street and toward the building.

"Okay, now I'm giving up," Mark groaned. "We've been at this for hours."

Nora looked over her shoulder at him. He was sitting in one chair with his feet up on another that he'd taken from the office next door. He was halfway through a recent edition of *Computer Science* and a Snickers bar. Yeah, these past few hours had been really rough on him.

"Do you want to find the program or not?"

"I'm thinking I would have better luck finding Santos at this point. Are you sure you haven't missed it?"

"I haven't missed it. There's nothing of any significance on anything I checked." It made her think, though. There was nothing of any significance at all. Not only couldn't she find the "magic" program, all the standard encryption work he would have been doing wasn't there, either. If Denny wasn't saving any of his work on memory sticks, then it was a good bet that he was saving it somewhere else. She was about to suggest another course of action when a knock on Denny's open door got their attention.

The security officer from downstairs stood in the doorway with a pensive look on his face.

"Can we help you?" Mark asked.

"I don't know if it matters to you but it seemed strange," the older man began. "Mrs. Santos came in to get a picture from Mr. Santos's office."

"Caroline Santos," Mark said pushing one chair back and leaping to his feet. "She's here?"

"Yes, she said she wanted a picture. She was really upset. I thought it would be okay. But Mr. Santos's office is on the fifteenth floor and the elevator stopped at the tenth."

Mark and Nora exchanged a glance. Instantly Nora rolled back from the workstation and followed Mark at dead run down the hall.

Which really wasn't easy in three-inch platform heels.

Caroline checked the map hastily drawn on the bag. She stopped in front of a closed metal door and used the security code Dominic had given her. A light on the panel flashed green. She opened the door to find a small room with a tower of what appeared to be stacked computers enclosed behind glass. Lights flickered and wires ran from every orifice, but as Dominic said it was the only one in the room.

She opened the glass door and spotted the Eject button. She hit it and immediately heard a whirling noise until the cartridge popped out.

She snatched it up and quickly left following the hall back to the elevators when the *click, click* sound of someone running stopped her. Turning, she saw two forms at the other end of the corridor. A man and a shorter woman.

"What are you doing here, Caroline?" Mark shouted down the long hallway.

There wasn't a good answer to that. Logic told her to walk toward them, hand them the cartridge and let them find what they were looking for, but instinct had her rooted to where she stood.

Adrenaline flooded her system. This wasn't supposed to happen, she and Dominic needed the answers first and then they could go to the police. If they were caught now

Dominic would be put in a cell. A cell he'd already told her that he didn't know if could handle. She had to protect him. Had to try.

Panicked and uncertain, she bolted.

Clutching the small tape in her hand, she turned and sprinted in the opposite direction. She found another corridor and turned, having no real idea where she was going. But when she reached the end of the hallway she spotted a red sign marked EXIT. She pushed against the door and immediately started down the metal stairs as fast as she could. She'd made it three flights, then stopped to catch her breath. She could hear clicking from above now.

"Caroline, you don't have to run. We're trying to help," Nora shouted down to her, her voice a little wheezy.

Caroline looked up and saw Nora leaning over the rail, gasping for breath.

"You have to let me get him out of here," Caroline shouted, hearing the desperation in her voice echo in the stairwell. "Then I'll give you what you need. All of it, but you can't bring him in."

"He doesn't have a choice," Nora said. "Not now. He needs to talk to us so we can end this."

No. Caroline couldn't let it happen. She needed to get to Dominic, needed to make him go, then she would hand over the tape and tell Nora what to do. She picked up her speed, taking the stairs two at a time and heard a loud curse as someone fell over above her.

"Damn heels!"

The large L printed on the door came into view and Caroline reached for the metal bar that ran across it. Hurtling into the lobby, she was ready to outrun the security guard, too, if he'd still been there. She threw the glass doors to the building open and stopped as soon as she hit the sidewalk.

The rain poured down around her and instinctively, she shoved the cartridge down the front of her jeans to protect it.

Too late. She was too late.

Dominic was spread-eagled over the hood of her BMW. Mark stood behind him, snapping a second cuff into place. She couldn't hear what he was saying, but she saw Mark's lips moving and she knew Dominic had just been read his Miranda rights.

Something inside her snapped. This was wrong. This wasn't the way it was supposed to happen. He was innocent and she couldn't let him go to jail. She wouldn't let him go to jail. She wouldn't lose him again.

He was her family.

"Let him go!"

Taken aback by her shrill scream, Mark lifted his head and stepped away from the car. He felt two flat palms hit his chest with a power that stunned him and sent him stumbling back another few feet. He had to work to keep from falling on his butt.

"What the hell?" He hadn't expected this from Caroline. Nora, maybe, but not Caroline.

"Caroline, stop it!" Dominic shouted at her as she geared up for another attack.

"Take the cuffs off!" she screamed, so ferociously that Mark considered reaching for his weapon.

"Caroline!" Dominic yelled again. He managed to lift himself from the hood of the car and positioned himself in front of his wife.

"They can't do this," she said, her eyes closed and her fists clenched. "I won't let them."

Mark raised his eyebrows. He wondered how she

thought she was going to pull that off, but let it go since it seemed Dominic was talking her down from the ledge.

"It's all right. You'll follow me to the station."

She reached for his face, ridiculously trying to wipe away the rain from his cheeks. The look on her face. Damn, Mark thought. When he got married, in like thirty or forty years, he wanted his wife to gaze at him just like that.

"I got the tape," she whispered to him.

"Good," he said. "We'll give it to the police. It will be okay."

"He doesn't have to be handcuffed," she snapped at him.

Mark blinked. "Yeah, but I'm thinking you do. Look, I have to take him in for questioning. He's wanted. He shouldn't have run and he knows it. Now back off and let me do my job. The sooner all this is settled, the better it will be. For both of you."

By that time Nora had managed to puff her way across the street, her shoes now smartly in her hands instead of on her feet.

"Wow, you're really out of shape. You need to work out more," Mark told her while she bent over to suck in air.

"Are you kidding me?" She huffed. "You took the elevator!"

Chapter 17

"You can't put him in a cell."

Nora pushed a disposable cup into her sort-of sister-in-law's hand. "Mark isn't the enemy. He wants to find the person who did it, not just make an arrest. He's good police."

Caroline took the drink but didn't respond. The two wet women sat on a bench in the precinct's lobby. Cops and criminals, lawyers and victims, came and went. It was late at night, but it could have been the middle of the afternoon so busy was the station.

"Can I ask a question?" Nora wasn't big on long silences.

Caroline nodded once.

"What made you stick with him? I mean, I was there when you found out about his past. And then you took off for Virginia and I figured I couldn't blame you, but something must have brought you back."

"I didn't come back alone," Caroline corrected her.

"Dominic was waiting for me at my house. That's where he was hiding. He called me, told me to go home. I thought he was sending me away, but he wasn't."

"So you came back with him. You didn't have to."

"No. I insisted. I came with him because I wanted to prove his innocence." Caroline shifted in her seat. "I came because I love him."

Nora smiled. She wasn't sure why because she and Dominic really weren't that close, but it made her glad to know that this woman would stick by him. "I thought so. You looked like a woman in love."

Caroline snorted. "I'm not the sort of person who falls in love at first sight. Too cowardly to ever take a risk like that. But there was something about him. I don't know. When I saw his picture for the first time, I thought he looked lonely. Don't tell him I said that. I think he would hate it. I stared at the photo for hours. I had this idea that I could be good for him."

"You will be. When all this is straightened out. Dominic needs someone. He's always needed someone. He certainly wouldn't let it be me…" Nora stopped. "Oh, I didn't mean…. We weren't an item or anything we just worked together."

"I know you're his sister," Caroline said.

"Wow. He told you." Nora felt a rush of something swamp her. She always understood why he'd wanted to keep their secret. He needed to guard the links to his past. He gave her a job, a life really, so she couldn't begrudge him it. But keeping the secret had made her feel marginal to him. Nora doubted he had a choice in telling Caroline, but still she felt connected to him now. More than she ever had before.

"So I guess this means we're like sisters."

Slowly they turned toward each other. "I never had a sister," Caroline whispered, her eyes watering.

"Me, neither," Nora concurred feeling choked up herself. "Maybe we can go shopping together. For shoes or something."

"I would like that."

"Okay, then. It's a date." Nora smiled. "You know, right after we prove Dominic's innocence."

Suddenly the good feelings were gone as the enormity of the situation reasserted itself.

"He can't go to jail," Caroline muttered. Nora reached out and took her hand. "He can't."

Dominic sat in a hard metal chair in the interrogation room. The room was spartan. Two chairs, one table and the standard two-way mirror. There were no windows.

He knew he was being made to wait to increase his feelings of isolation and fear, and already the claustrophobia was creeping up on him. He fought it off. He couldn't be afraid for himself. Not any longer.

Only Caroline occupied his thoughts. If he couldn't fix this, if he couldn't prove Steven had killed Denny, then his only choices were to run or go to jail. Either way, Caroline would suffer.

Because she loved him. Whether she wanted to or not.

That fact sure as hell bothered him more than any small room.

The door opened and the detective who had introduced himself as Mark Hernandez entered.

"How are you holding up?" Hernandez asked.

Good cop, Dominic identified immediately. "How do you think I'm holding up?"

"You need anything to drink?"

"No."

"You kill Denny Haskell?"

Dominic stared at the detective. "No."

"Who did?"

"You're the detective, you tell me."

"I think you did it."

Dominic met the man's eyes again. "No, you don't."

Mark pulled the empty chair away from the table, the sound of the metal skidding along the floor echoed. He straddled it and folded his arms against the back. "Yeah, you're right. I don't."

"I sent an e-mail…"

"I know all about the e-mail to Nora. That means jack in my book. She's a computer whiz and she's doing everything to convince me that you're innocent. Do you know about your secretary?"

Dominic's brow furrowed. "Serena? What about her?"

"She's dead."

The news was too sudden, told too quickly, without enough preparation. Dominic sucked air into his lungs and tried to wrap his mind around the idea of what that actually meant. Serena dead. Serena. Dead.

"Who? How?"

"Well, conventional wisdom around this place says it happened like this. You were stealing money from your own company. Haskell found out about it and confronted you, so you sneaked out of your office. You followed him in your Mercedes, pushed him off the cliff, dumped the car somewhere, then snuck back into your own office so the cameras could tag you leaving in the morning. But then you got nervous, decided to take some ready cash out of the bank and went into hiding. After a time, you realized that your secretary might also be aware of or have proof of your embezzlement scheme so you offed her, too. It was another car accident and there were more paint chips from the same Mercedes."

"Why would I steal money from a profitable company I owned?"

"I'm supposed to be asking the questions."

"You haven't asked me anything yet," Dominic pointed out.

"I'm getting to it," Mark snapped. "You know I'm starting to see a resemblance between you and that sister of yours."

Dominic's brow lifted.

"Yeah, I know about that, too. I know about your record. I know about your father. And I know what you did for Nora."

There was nothing to say, so Dominic remained silent.

"Were you planning to embezzle two million dollars but got caught before you could?"

"No."

"When did you discover the books had been altered?"

"That night. When I saw that the figures had been changed, I thought it was a mistake. Or a joke. I didn't know what the hell it was. After Steven called me, I quickly understood that I was being set up. Because of my past I couldn't take the chance that anyone, especially the police, would believe me. I ran."

"Tell me about this program you needed to come back here to get your hands on. The one you told Nora about."

"It's very dangerous. In the wrong hands it could mean disaster."

"You think Denny was killed because of it."

"It's the only explanation," Dominic answered. "He told somebody about it. I know that much. I think he was killed to stop him from telling anyone else."

Mark shook his head. "Haskell's killing wasn't spur of

the moment. The financial statements were changed before Denny was killed. Whoever did this had a plan. Two birds. One stone."

And now Dominic knew that Serena had been involved in that setup. She would have had access to his files. She could have replaced the real statements with the doctored ones. It hurt him to know that she had betrayed him, almost as much as the news of her death.

"I bet you think that person is Steven Ford," Mark suggested.

"Yes," Dominic said tightly, the word sticking like a chicken bone in his throat.

"Why?"

"A third of the company wasn't enough for him. He must have wanted it all. I would never have approved the development of Denny's program. Never. If he knew that and wanted to get me and Denny out of the picture, this was the way to do it. Two birds. One stone. His company."

Hernandez stood. "I'm going to go call Steven. Bring him down here for questioning. In the meantime, I'm putting you in a holding cell. You can call a lawyer."

"I don't need a lawyer yet."

"Fine. But you'll sit tight until I hear what Ford has to say about this. That's the way it's got to be."

Dominic nodded.

"When your wife finds out I'm not ready to let you go, she's going to hit me again, isn't she?"

For the first time in a long time Dominic felt his lips twitching into a smile. "Yes, she probably is."

The detective headed for the door, then stopped. "As far as you know did Denny have a girlfriend?"

"A girlfriend? No. You have to know Denny. He wasn't very socially adept." Dominic stared at his hands and then a memory came to him. "Wait. Caroline said something to me. When we were arguing about something else. She said there was office talk about Denny having a crush on someone. I didn't believe it. Figured it was just gossip."

Hernandez's eyes drifted off, and Dominic felt as if he were putting something together.

"I'll be back."

Mark stopped in front of the two women who seemed to be leaning against each other for support.

"Why don't you both go home?"

Caroline stared at him. "I'm not leaving without Dominic."

"Look, this is going to take a while. He's got to stay here until I get a few things sorted out. There's no point in you sitting up all night."

"I'm not—"

"Leaving," he finished. "Stubborn and violent. Hey, shortcake, wake up." Mark bumped Nora's leg with his foot. She immediately popped her head up.

"What? I wasn't sleeping."

"Take Mrs. Santos home. It is Mrs. Santos?"

"It is," Caroline agreed.

Mark crouched down. "Listen, I understand you want to be loyal and stick by your man. But you're not doing him any good by sitting here in a hard chair not getting any sleep. Go back to the house. Take a hot bath, do whatever it is women do. Then you come back tomorrow and you'll be ready for whatever's next."

"What's next?" she asked wearily.

"I don't know. But I want the truth, Caroline, even if that's not the easy answer."

He hated the doubt he saw in her eyes.

"Trust me," Mark urged her.

"I told you," Nora interrupted. "He's not the worst detective in the world. I think we can trust him."

Mark stood up and smiled down at his pint-sized partner. "You know, shortcake, you keep talking like that I'm going to think you like me."

"I'll be extra careful, then. Come on, Caroline. Let's get out of here."

Nora got Caroline to her feet and guided her to the station's doors.

Abruptly they both stopped. Mark wondered what was up until he saw the station's newest arrival.

Steven Ford had just walked through the door.

"Caroline!" Steven called out rushing up to her. "Is it true? Is Dominic here? Is he okay?"

"Get away from me," Caroline told him.

Mark saw her reach for Nora's arm and hold on tight.

"Let's get out of here. Now." Caroline moved around him and Nora followed. Together they left arm in arm.

"Caroline." Clearly the man was confused. "I don't understand. Wait."

Mark watched the interaction. "Let them go," he said as he approached Ford.

"I don't understand. What's happening? I want to see Dominic."

"First things first. I've got a few more questions I would like to ask you." Mark steered him in the direction of a hallway that led to the interrogation room. He opened the door and allowed him to walk in of his own accord.

"What is this?" he asked. "Where's Dominic?"

"Have a seat Mr. Ford. I have to tell you that if you would like, you may call your lawyer."

"I don't want a damn lawyer. I want to know what this is about."

"This is about the death of Denny Haskell and Serena Almonde."

"Serena?" Steven whispered. He reached for the chair and dropped into it. "No, that's not possible."

"The police found her in her car a few hours ago, I'm afraid. She was killed sometime early yesterday afternoon."

"How?"

"Car ran her off the road into a tree."

The man winced at the news.

"Where were you around noon yesterday, Mr. Ford?"

Steven gulped a few times and blinked his eyes, as if he couldn't stop himself.

"I was at the office," he finally said.

"Can you think of any reason why someone would want to kill Serena?"

"I still can't think of a reason why someone would want to kill Denny!" he shouted back. "None of this makes sense."

Just then, a discreet knock sounded at the door. Mark got up as a uniform officer slipped him a piece of paper, then quickly retreated.

Mark read the paper then looked at Steven and decided to play a hunch. "You can't think of any reason why someone might want to kill Denny?"

"No."

"Mr. Ford, did you know your wife was having an affair with him?"

Dominic sat in a corner of the large holding cell. He tried to tell himself that it wasn't the same as a real cell, but it didn't work. The bars were just as solid, the loss of freedom equally powerful. Whoever had created the cell knew what they were doing when it came to psychological torture. A man inside lost his dignity, his liberty and his ego. A man inside a cell was never the same as the man outside.

To take his mind off of his location, Dominic closed his eyes and tried to think. Serena was dead. Murdered. What had motivated her to get involved in all of this? He had to assume it was money. What had Caroline told him, something about some family she was trying to get into the States? At least he could pretend her motivation stemmed from desperation.

Steven's motive was less clear.

Dominic mapped out the events in his mind. Steven must have learned about the program that Denny had created, saw its potential and decided that he wanted it all for himself. So he altered the books, had Serena make the switch, killed Denny and then just waited for everything else to play out.

Only the money was still in the company's account. So if it was a setup, it was a poor one. If Dominic didn't have the kind of past he did, he might not have run. Then it would have been his word against Steven's as to how the books got altered. Not exactly a sure thing.

Was it possible Denny told him about their shared criminal past? Dominic couldn't see Denny revealing himself like that to Steven. The two men weren't close at all, barely spoke to one another.

It was odd, Dominic mused. Steven had plenty of money from his share of the company's profits despite repaying his loan to Russell. Of the three of them, he was really the least ambitious. If it wasn't for his father-in-law's influence, he might have never thought of becoming a partner. So what the hell was he planning to do with the program once he got it?

* * *

"Denny?"

Mark watched the man's reaction. He saw shock and disbelief. But that didn't mean a whole lot to him. Most criminals could fake shock and disbelief pretty easily.

"It's not possible."

"Denny had your number in his cell phone."

"That doesn't mean anything."

"Phone records indicate he called your house the night he was killed. My guess is he spoke to your wife. Is that what set you off? Did you hear her on the phone with him and crack?"

"Don't be ridiculous! It's not possible. Anne hated Denny. He disgusted her."

"Disgust. That's a pretty powerful word. If it's true, then it's odd that we found a magazine with her fingerprints in his office. Remember we printed everyone connected to this case to eliminate familiar prints. Strange place to find your wife's, though. Can you think of any reason she would spend time in his office?"

Steven opened, then closed his mouth.

Mark pulled the empty chair close to him so he could look the man in the face. "Let me ask you something, Steven. As far as you know has your wife ever strayed before?"

For a split second, Steven's eyes sharpened into angry slits. It was all the answer Mark needed. "I'm sorry. I truly am. Who was he?"

"Dominic Santos," Steven muttered thickly.

"Can I just say you were completely off base."

Dominic immediately jumped to his feet as he heard the detective make his way down the row of cells.

"This wasn't about your fancy computer program at

all," Hernandez said, even as he reached down to unlock the door. "This was about the second-greatest motive for murder. Revenge. Plain and simple."

"What are you saying?" Dominic struggled to catch up. "Steven wanted revenge? Against me?"

"You and Denny. But not for the reason you might think. Let me ask you something, Santos. You ever have an affair with Anne Ford?"

Slowly, Dominic sank back down on the holding cell bench.

"It wasn't an affair," Dominic mumbled. "It was a pass. That was it. Nothing happened."

"She made a play for you, though. Not something you would be thrilled to know about your wife. Then she does the other partner and…"

"Anne and Denny? That's not possible."

"So everyone tells me. But I found a magazine in Denny's office with her prints all over it. There was Ford's home number in Denny's cell. A call made to his house from said phone. And right now, the jilted husband is in the interrogation room crying like a baby."

"He confessed?"

"No, but I think it's just a matter of time," Mark figured. "The pieces fit. He wanted to get back at Denny for shacking up with his wife. He wanted to get back at you for being someone his wife hit on. Denny's dead. You're in jail. He keeps the company for himself and probably ditches the wife."

Dominic considered the theory, but it was hard to swallow. "You have to know Anne. It just doesn't seem like her to have an affair with someone like Denny."

"Yeah, Ford thought he disgusted her, but you never know what goes on in a woman's mind. Take Nora, for instance.

What type of guy do you think she would be attracted to? Not that I care. I'm just trying to make a point here."

But Dominic ignored the question. Anne and Denny. Anne hated his scruffiness. She hated the way he endlessly talked about his programs. She hated Denny. So what made her get in bed with him? Was she trying to get back at Steven for something?

No.

A stillness crept over Dominic and he suddenly he could hear his heart beat, hear the sound of his breath entering and leaving his body. "You were right," he told the detective who was still rambling on about Nora's taste in men.

He stopped when Dominic spoke. "Right about what?"

"This wasn't about the program."

"I told *you* that."

"This was about revenge."

"Yeah, I know. Keep up. Ford took revenge against the men who his wife obviously wanted more than him."

"No," Dominic said bursting out of the cell as soon as the door swung open. "This is about revenge. But not Steven's."

Chapter 18

"An indoor pool. A house on the beach. A bestselling sister-in-law. I'm really going to have to start visiting more."

Caroline smiled at Nora, who immediately made herself comfortable on the couch.

It did feel good to be home. And this was home. She knew it. It was the difference between the dread she'd felt standing inside the foyer of her house in Leesburg and the hope she felt now. Steven was in police custody, the truth would come out and it would be over.

As soon as Dominic walked through the door, she was going to propose to him.

She thought of their first wedding in Vegas. Quick. Efficient. She hadn't wanted anything else. Plus, she didn't think he would have gone for it if she had.

Things were different now. There was honesty. Openness. She wasn't going to be polite about what she wanted out of their marriage anymore. Her days of walking on egg-shells were over. The coward inside her was officially dead.

She thought about how Dominic admired her serenity. She wondered how he would feel about her fire.

"You ever been a bridesmaid, Nora?"

Nora's brow lifted in an exact imitation of Dominic's. "You thinking of putting a big pink bow on my ass?"

Caroline laughed. "Maybe not pink."

"I'm in. Anything that makes him happy. I'm in."

"Because you think you owe him," Caroline said. "You know he probably wouldn't like that."

"Can't help it. I do. He gave me my life back."

"You know he came to see you. When you graduated from the academy, he was there. And one of the reasons he wanted to win this government contract was so that he would have a chance to visit you more often. He was going to try."

Nora's surprise was evident, and her slow smile told its own story. "Thanks. For letting me know. If I start calling him bro, do you think it will freak him out?"

"I do," Caroline replied. "And I think you absolutely should. I'm going to go for a swim to try and work off all this extra adrenaline. You want to join me?"

"As in exercise? Tonight? I already had to run to chase you down a flight of stairs. That's enough physical activity for me for a week." Nora found the remote and began flicking through the channels on the flat-screen.

"If you get tired there's a guest room upstairs."

"I'm cool. My bet is Hernandez will either call or stop by once he has news."

After changing into her suit, Caroline made her way to the pool, switching on the underwater lights but opting to leave the rest of the room in the dark. She'd found that way she could see the stars more clearly. The rain clouds were finally passing and the stars in the night sky twinkled.

She took pleasure in diving into the water in one clean leap. Hands piercing the surface. Body plunging afterward. No thought. No hesitation.

The water greeted her like a warm massage. She wondered how long she could stay under water. How long could she escape from the noise. How long could she continue to fly. Not too long.

Halfway to the other end of the pool, she kicked off the bottom and found air. Sucking it into her lungs, she dove under once more, determined to swim the rest of the length of the pool. She focused on the light shining from the center of the stairs underneath the water.

Suddenly the lamp went out and she poked her head up. Her first assumption was that the bulb had gone.

That assumption was wrong.

"Hello, Caroline."

"Anne." She huffed, trying to recover the air she'd denied her lungs. "What are you doing here?" Caroline didn't hesitate and climbed the stairs out of the pool.

Anne held a towel out for her. Carefully Caroline took it as ideas ran through her head. She must know about Steven. Maybe he'd already been charged with murder. It was certainly enough to make a wife angry. Desperate. Caroline knew.

Feeling vulnerable and slightly exposed in the bathing suit, she wrapped the towel around her breasts and slicked the wet hair off her face. "What are you doing here?" Caroline asked again.

Anne simply smiled. "I hear Dominic's back. You must be thrilled."

"I am." She didn't have to wonder what the strange sensation swirling throughout her body was. It consumed her and turned her knees to mush. It was her old friend, fear. "Did Nora let you in?"

Cautiously, Caroline turned her head, but she couldn't see up to where the couch was on the second level.

"Yes, she's upstairs watching TV. She told me you were down here."

The feeling rolling through her gut increased, accompanied by a roaring in her ears. Nora wouldn't have sent this woman downstairs. She would have wanted to know what the hell she was doing here in the first place and why she wasn't down at police headquarters supporting her husband.

Anne had done something to Nora. It was the only explanation. And it explained everything else.

"You and Steven are in this together."

"Wrong!" Anne shouted and then chortled arrogantly. "Come on, Caroline. You're a mystery writer. Surely, you can do better than that. Steven? You think he was behind this? Please. Steven couldn't find his way to the executive washroom if I didn't lead him there."

Caroline took a step back. "I'm not in the mood to play games, Anne."

"But aren't you curious? I mean you're going to die, Caroline. Don't you want to know why?"

It wasn't until she actually said the word *die* that Caroline saw the gun in the woman's hand bumping against her hip. Focusing on the glint of steel, she couldn't look away.

"Ask me," Anne insisted.

"Why?" It was barely a whisper because there was no saliva left in her mouth.

"Well, there's Denny's program. It's going to be very useful to me when I take over the company. Daddy says we're going to make more money than we have ever dreamed of."

"Russell's involved, too."

"He knows about the program. He just doesn't know *everything* I had to do to get it. And I did have to do a lot. The money I'm going to make will be my reward. In fact, I don't know that all of this would have been worth it otherwise." Then Anne seemed to reconsider that statement. "Or maybe it would have been. I'm not sure. Actually this has all been rather exciting for me. I had always heard that revenge could be sweet, but I didn't know it could be fun, too."

"Revenge against me for what?" Caroline asked. "I barely know you."

"Not against you. Dominic, silly. Maybe you weren't aware of this, but your husband did something no one else has ever done."

"Rejection hurts," Caroline said remembering what Anne had said about never being denied.

"I *really* don't like it," she said.

Caroline started thinking about escape. There had been no gunshot, so whatever she'd done to Nora, she hadn't shot her. If she'd surprised her somehow, knocked her out, maybe she was recovering and calling for help. She had to believe that because physically she didn't match up with Anne. The woman had arms forged like steel. There was only one place where they might fight as equals.

"I just couldn't have it. I mean, look at me, Caroline. If Dominic was going to have either one of us, clearly I'm the logical choice."

"Clearly," Caroline muttered, her eyes once again falling to the gun. "So this all began when Dominic married me?"

"No. Before then. Right after he turned me away. You see, Daddy always taught me never to take no for an answer. That's how you get what you want in life. But that wasn't working with Dominic. It made me very angry. So

I decided if I couldn't have him, I would take the one thing he cared about most."

"His company."

Anne beamed. "Bingo."

She was getting close to the end of her story. There was no sound from upstairs. Caroline was going to have to act soon.

"I started sleeping with Denny. Let me tell you what a chore that was, but it was the only way I could get the information I needed about Dominic. You see, Denny and Dominic knew each other long before Steven came along. I found out all about Dominic's nefarious past and that's when I decided how I would get even."

"Doesn't seem fair to Denny."

"No, I suppose it wasn't. And naturally he almost ruined everything by telling Dominic what he was working on. I wanted to have the program in my hand before I did anything. Not that it mattered. Denny had to die because by doing so, his shares in the company reverted to Steven and Dominic. I fixed the books to make it look like Dominic was embezzling money, then had the files saved on his hard drive. Serena was very helpful for the low, low price of one hundred thousand dollars. Turns out her niece back in Mexico was sick, poor thing. The visa for her brother was taking too long, so Serena was going to use the money to hire a coyote to smuggle her brother and niece across the border. I actually considered letting her keep the money, but of course I couldn't. She knew too much."

Caroline wanted to throw up as the woman casually rattled off her reasons for the multiple murders.

"Dominic goes back to jail, a very fitting revenge. He sells his shares to Steven to save the company. I produce a child that guarantees the company gets passed to us. I really mean to me. And I win. The one thing I didn't count on was…"

"Me," Caroline answered.

"You. You get pregnant and maybe Dominic doesn't sell his shares. You have a baby and I have to share the company. I don't like to share. The plan was to get you out of the way first, but, like I said, Denny ruined all that. If you had gone home and not come back, I could have spared you. I'm not a monster, Caroline. I've already gotten everything I want. But then Steven said you were both back, and well, you need to die. Sorry." Anne shrugged as if she truly were.

"Steven is down at police headquarters right now. They know Dominic didn't kill Denny. You've lost. You can't possibly hope to avoid being caught."

"Not if Dominic comes home and kills his wife and the FBI agent with her in a fit of rage because he truly is a twisted psychopath. I've heard prison can do that to a man. Then he kills himself and we're back to square one. You're a mystery writer, Caroline. You know how it's done. You need evidence. You can't arrest anyone without it. There is no proof that Steven killed anyone. And there is no proof that I did. Maybe people will have their suspicions, but there won't be anything they can do about it. We're going to go upstairs and wait for Dominic to come home and when he does, this is all finally going to play out. Lucky for me Daddy is at this moment taking a woman I set him up with—one who, coincidentally, looks very much like me—out on the town where a number of security cameras are sure to provide me with a solid alibi." Anne shook the gun in her hand, indicating that Caroline should walk. "Go on. Let's just get this over with."

Yes. Over. Caroline took a deep breath and started to walk as if she were heading back into the house. Then at the last second she turned and threw herself at Anne.

Caroline had momentum and the element of surprise on her side. Both women plunged deep into the dark water.

"I have to talk to Steven." Dominic told Mark. He must have conveyed his panic to the detective because Mark nodded his head once and escorted him back to the inter-rogation room.

Steven was still sitting there, looking as if his world had just crumbled around him. He might have seemed excep-tionally guilty, too, but Dominic knew he wasn't.

"Steven."

The man turned around with a jerk and stared at Dominic. "I saw it happen. It was at that stupid Hallow-een party she threw last year. She wanted you. I could practically smell it on her. Then I saw her lead you down the hall to one of the back bedrooms and I couldn't make myself follow you because I knew I would lose her."

"I'm sorry you saw that. I didn't know." Dominic walked over and sat across from him. "Nothing happened."

"I know. She was so furious when she rejoined the party. Said it was because the caterer messed up, but I knew. You had turned her down. She doesn't handle no very well."

Dominic closed his eyes. "You know, don't you?"

Steven nodded and dropped his head between his hands. He chuckled hysterically for a minute and Dominic rested a hand on his shoulder to calm him. "Don't you see? This is so like her. She's so intense. Everything at full speed. Even her anger. Her revenge."

"Where is she now?" Mark wanted to know.

"I left her at home. I told her you were back. That you'd been arrested and I had to come down and see what I could do. She said she would wait by the phone." Steven's breath caught in his throat. "She slept with Denny. She slept with him just to make all this happen."

"Call her," Mark prompted. "Tell her you need her to come down here to verify your alibi. Tell her the police suspect you and you need her help."

Steven pulled out his cell phone and gripped it tightly in his hand. He looked up at the two men watching him and whispered, "She's my wife."

"She's a murderer," Mark told him coldly. "Make the call or we go and pick her up in a squad car."

Steven hit a button and held the phone to his ear. "No answer at home."

"Try her cell."

"She never answers her cell. She said she'd be at home. Maybe she's not answering."

"I'm not taking that chance," Dominic insisted. He turned to the detective. "I need to go to Caroline. Now."

The two men looked at each other. Then immediately bolted into action.

"You sit tight. I'm going to send a uniform in here to wait with you," Mark told Steven. Once that was done, Mark led the way out of the station and pointed to his car.

"I'm driving," Dominic insisted.

Mark jingled the keys in his hands. "I'm driving. You're about half gone with panic."

"I swear to God if anything happens to her…" Dominic muttered as he threw himself into the passenger seat and silently urged the detective to move faster.

"Nora's with her and she'll be armed. And even if she weren't, I think I would still put my money on her."

* * *

Nora rolled on to her back and groaned. Her head felt as if it were going to explode. For a moment, she wondered if maybe it had. No, that was silly. If it had exploded, she'd be dead. And dead people didn't groan. Which she did again.

Think, she told herself. But that hurt.

All she really wanted to do was close her eyes and try to escape the pain, but there was the niggling anxiety in the back of her mind that wouldn't let her rest. A feeling of danger and an urgency to move spurred her on.

Move where, though? Where was she?

Dominic's house. She was at Dominic's house with Caroline.

Caroline. Where was Caroline? Had she hit her? No. There was someone else in the house. Oh, God.

"Caroline." She knew her voice couldn't be more than a whisper, but suddenly she realized that the urgency she was feeling was related to Caroline. She had to make contact. She crawled for while along the living room heading for the stairs that would take her down to the next level. Caroline had gone swimming. She should be in the pool.

That was confirmed by the sound of a very loud splash.

The water engulfed them both instantly. But because she knew where she was going, Caroline was able to adapt more quickly. She kicked away from the tangle that was Anne and felt something solid brush past her thigh.

The gun! Anne had dropped it and it was sinking. Caroline kicked her legs powerfully, pushing herself to the bottom of the pool. She brushed her hands over the tiles but with the underwater light turned off, she could see nothing.

Needing air, she rose to the surface. Only the glint of the moonlight peeking through the passing clouds offered any light inside the glass room. She couldn't see much, but she could hear Anne breathing.

"You bitch!"

Caroline remained motionless as the woman floundered about struggling with her clothes. Instead of bothering to reply Caroline dove again and with fluid strokes moved farther away from her. Once more, she kicked her way to the bottom of the pool, holding her breath as long as possible in her desperate search for the gun. She heard a muted sound and felt a hand close around her ankle. She kicked sharply and dislodged the hand, then kicked again, angling her body to the side to change her direction.

As she surfaced, the ragged sound of her breathing gave Caroline's position away. Anne turned dramatically in her direction but she didn't move as a cloud obscuring the moon plunged the room into darkness.

Anne chuckled. "Marco," she sang as if waiting for the answering call, *Polo*. Caroline shivered.

Caroline needed that gun. The pool was large and the gun could be anywhere, but the most likely place was not too far from where they had both fallen into the water. Which meant she needed to get behind where Anne was standing.

"I'm here, Anne."

Instantly the woman lunged in her direction. Caroline sank deep and could feel the movement of the water above her. When they surfaced, Anne was on the other side of the pool.

Without a sound Caroline let herself slide back under the water. Her foot brushed a solid object and she twisted her body around, clasping the weapon in her hand. She kicked off the bottom and charged for the top.

She heard splashing behind her as she ran along the shallow end of the pool. She knew Anne was closing in on her, reaching for her. If she could just get the advantage of dry ground. Caroline climbed up the stairs, slipping on the slick stones and then turned around and fired the gun once into the air.

The crack and the jolt of the weapon's impact sent her sprawling backward and she fell butt-first on the edge of the pool. Quickly she spotted Anne still waist-deep in water and aimed at her.

"You think you have what it takes to shoot me?" Anne taunted.

Caroline continued to point the gun, but she could feel her hands shaking. "I don't want to kill you, Anne. Just give up."

"Give up? I don't think you've been listening very well. I. Don't. Give. Up." Anne had made her way to the stairs and was emerging out of the water like Poseidon. "You're going to have to shoot me to stop me. All you have to do is pull the trigger."

Shoot her. Just shoot her. Caroline raised the gun, felt her finger curling around the trigger. All she had to do was pull it. Pull the trigger and save Dominic and herself. Her family.

"What's the matter?" Anne sneered. "You can't do it, can you? Coward."

Caroline could see the woman was getting ready to jump when a light burst into the room, blinding them both for a second.

"Maybe she won't shoot you, but I will." Nora stood at the edge of the pool with a gun aimed directly at Anne. Blood dripped down her face and Caroline feared she would topple over at any second, but her gun hand didn't shake.

Caroline dropped her head in relief, then heard the pounding of feet as Mark and Dominic rushed into the pool room. Dominic was bearing down on her and she felt like a football as she was scooped up into his arms.

"Ughh!" Anne shouted, slapping her hands on the water with fury. "No, no, no, no! This isn't how it's supposed to be. I don't lose. I don't ever lose!"

"This time you do," Caroline said, her arms wrapped around Dominic's neck. "Take me away from her. I don't want to look at her face."

Moments later, uniformed officers swarmed the pool room. One kept his gun on the woman, while two entered the water. As they forcibly dragged her out, she kicked, screamed, and splashed the whole way.

Nora lowered her weapon and holstered it. She walked over to where Mark stood with his hands on his hips and a grim expression on his face. He reached out and swiped a stream of blood off her cheek.

"What the hell happened to you?"

"She snuck up on me. She must have been inside the house when we got here. One second I'm watching TV, the next I wake up sprawled out on the floor."

"Come here." He reached out and pulled her close, gently feeling her head for the lump she knew he would easily find.

"Ouch!" she hissed.

"We've got to have you checked out."

In a sudden motion, he bent and lifted her into his arms. She was about to do the proud thing and tell him she could manage on her own, but bereft of all energy, she let herself be carried through the house and outside to the ambulance that had been called to the scene.

The truth was, it felt kind of nice.

He sat her on the back of the ambulance and waved over the EMTs.

"When you get out of the hospital, we're going to work

on your surveillance skills. They suck. An elephant could sneak up on you."

"Screw you, Hernandez," she muttered weakly.

"Screw me? Eventually, shortcake," Mark replied smoothly. "Eventually."

Epilogue

"Dearly beloved. We are gathered here today to join this man and this woman in holy matrimony. To create, before God and guests, a family."

Mark glanced down at Nora's butt and smiled. "Psst. Glad you didn't get stuck with the bow."

"Shhh," she said. "I'm trying to pay attention. That's my brother up there."

"This is the boring the part," he told her. "It doesn't get good until the end."

This time she jabbed him in the ribs to shut him up. As her official date for this shindig, he supposed he had to take it.

"Do you, Caroline, take this man to be your lawfully wedded husband?"

"I do."

"Ah, gee," Mark whispered. "She's crying."

"Of course she's crying. She loves him," Nora hiccupped into a tissue.

"And do you, Dominic, take this woman to be your lawfully wedded wife?"

"I do."

"If he cries I'm outta here."

"If you don't shut up, you've got about a zero chance of getting hot wedding sex tonight." Nora gave him a final glare.

Mark took the threat seriously and quickly shut up. Although he didn't see what the big deal was. It wasn't as if these two hadn't been married before.

He got the gist of the event. Caroline loved Dominic. Dominic loved Caroline. And if that bump in the front of Caroline's wedding dress was any indication, it's not as if they had waited for wedding number two to get busy.

But wedding sex was wedding sex, and no man put that at risk. Add to that that this was going to be their first time and they were going to blow the doors and windows off the hotel room. Yep, no reason to rock that boat.

So he listened as the minister said the final words talking about what God had joined that no man could put asunder and so forth and so on. It was definitely a nice thing. Marriage. And in thirty or forty years, he definitely might give it a try.

Nora sniffed again and again, wiping her nose with the tissue. His eyes were drawn to the faint red mark that he remembered noticing the first time they met and he suddenly realized that he was looking at an old nose piercing. Huh.

Instantly his mind flashed to what else might have been

pierced. Or more importantly, what still might be. Short-cake was always going to be a surprise.

Thirty or forty years? Maybe ten or twenty.

* * * * *

*Celebrate 60 years of pure reading pleasure with
Harlequin®!*
*Silhouette® Romantic Suspense is celebrating with the
glamour-filled, adrenaline-charged series*
LOVE IN 60 SECONDS *starting in April 2009.*
*Six stories that promise to bring the glitz of Las Vegas,
the danger of revenge, the mystery of a missing diamond,
family scandals and ripped-from-the-headlines intrigue.
Get your heart racing as love happens in sixty seconds!*

Enjoy a sneak peek of
USA TODAY *bestselling author Marie Ferrarella's*
THE HEIRESS'S 2-WEEK AFFAIR
Available April 2009 from Silhouette® Romantic Suspense.

Eight years ago Matt Shaffer had vanished out of Natalie Rothchild's life, leaving behind a one-line note tucked under a pillow that had grown cold: *I'm sorry, but this just isn't going to work.*

That was it. No explanation, no real indication of remorse. The note had been as clinical and compassionless as an eviction notice, which, in effect, it had been, Natalie thought as she navigated through the morning traffic. Matt had written the note to evict her from his life.

She'd spent the next two weeks crying, breaking down without warning as she walked down the street, or as she sat staring at a meal she couldn't bring herself to eat.

Candace, she remembered with a bittersweet pang, had tried to get her to go clubbing in order to get her to forget about Matt.

She'd turned her twin down, but she did get her act

together. If Matt didn't think enough of their relationship to try to contact her, to try to make her understand why he'd changed so radically from lover to stranger, then to hell with him. He was dead to her, she resolved. And he'd remained that way.

Until twenty minutes ago.

The adrenaline in her veins kept mounting.

Natalie focused on her driving. Vegas in the daylight wasn't nearly as alluring, as magical and glitzy as it was after dark. Like an aging woman best seen in soft lighting, Vegas's imperfections were all visible in the daylight. Natalie supposed that was why people like her sister didn't like to get up until noon. They lived for the night.

Except that Candace could no longer do that.

The thought brought a fresh, sharp ache with it.

"Damn it, Candy, what a waste," Natalie murmured under her breath.

She pulled up before the Janus casino. One of the three valets currently on duty came to life and made a beeline for her vehicle.

"Welcome to the Janus," the young attendant said cheerfully as he opened her door with a flourish.

"We'll see," she replied solemnly.

As he pulled away with her car, Natalie looked up at the casino's logo. Janus was the Roman god with two faces, one pointed toward the past, the other facing the future. It struck her as rather ironic, given what she was doing here, seeking out someone from her past in order to get answers so that the future could be settled.

The moment she entered the casino, the Vegas phenomena took hold. It was like stepping into a world where time did not matter or even make an appearance. There was only a sense of "now."

Because in Natalie's experience she'd discovered that bartenders knew the inner workings of any establishment they worked for better than anyone else, she made her way to the first bar she saw within the casino.

The bartender in attendance was a gregarious man in his early forties. He had a quick, sexy smile, which was probably one of the main reasons he'd been hired. His name tag identified him as Kevin.

Moving to her end of the bar, Kevin asked, "What'll it be, pretty lady?"

"Information." She saw a dubious look cross his brow. To counter that, she took out her badge. Granted she wasn't here in an official capacity, but Kevin didn't need to know that. "Were you on duty last night?"

Kevin began to wipe the gleaming black surface of the bar. "You mean during the gala?"

"Yes."

The smile gracing his lips was a satisfied one. Last night had obviously been profitable for him, she judged. "I caught an extra shift."

She took out Candace's photograph and carefully placed it on the bar. "Did you happen to see this woman there?"

The bartender glanced at the picture. Mild interest turned to recognition. "You mean Candace Rothchild? Yeah, she was here, loud and brassy as always. But not for long," he added, looking rather disappointed. There was always a circus when Candace was around, Natalie thought. "She and the boss had at it and then he had our head of security escort her out."

She latched onto the first part of his statement. "They argued? About what?"

He shook his head. "Couldn't tell you. Too far away for anything but body language," he confessed.

"And the head of security?" she asked.

"He got her to leave."

She leaned in over the bar. "Tell me about him."

"Don't know much," the bartender admitted. "Just that his name's Matt Shaffer. Boss flew him in from L.A., where he was head of security for Montgomery Enterprises."

There was no avoiding it, she thought darkly. She was going to have to talk to Matt. The thought left her cold. "Do you know where I can find him right now?"

Kevin glanced at his watch. "He should be in his office. On the second floor, toward the rear." He gave her the numbers of the rooms where the monitors that kept watch over the casino guests as they tried their luck against the house were located.

Taking out a twenty, she placed it on the bar. "Thanks for your help."

Kevin slipped the bill into his vest pocket. "Anytime, lovely lady," he called after her. "Anytime."

She debated going up the stairs, then decided on the elevator. The car that took her up to the second floor was empty. Natalie stepped out of the elevator, looked around to get her bearings and then walked toward the rear of the floor.

"Into the Valley of Death rode the six hundred," she silently recited, digging deep for a line from a poem by Tennyson. Wrapping her hand around a brass handle, she opened one of the glass doors and walked in.

The woman whose desk was closest to the door looked up. "You can't come in here. This is a restricted area."

Natalie already had her ID in her hand and held it up. "I'm looking for Matt Shaffer," she told the woman.

God, even saying his name made her mouth go dry. She was supposed to be over him, to have moved on with her life. What happened?

The woman began to answer her. "He's—"

"Right here."

The deep voice came from behind her. Natalie felt every single nerve ending go on tactical alert at the same moment that all the hairs at the back of her neck stood up. Eight years had passed, but she would have recognized his voice anywhere.

* * * * *

Why did Matt Shaffer leave heiress-turned-cop Natalie Rothchild?
What does he know about the death of Natalie's twin sister?
Come and meet these two reunited lovers and learn the secrets of the Rothchild family in
THE HEIRESS'S 2-WEEK AFFAIR
by USA TODAY *bestselling author*
Marie Ferrarella.
The first book in Silhouette® Romantic Suspense's wildly romantic new continuity,
LOVE IN 60 SECONDS!
Available April 2009.

CELEBRATE
60 YEARS
OF PURE READING PLEASURE
WITH HARLEQUIN®!

Look for Silhouette®
Romantic Suspense in April!

Love In 60 Seconds

Bright lights. Big city. Hearts in overdrive.

Silhouette® Romantic Suspense is celebrating
Harlequin's 60th Anniversary with six stories that
promise to bring readers the glitz of Las Vegas,
the danger of revenge, the mystery of a missing
diamond, and family scandals.

**Look for the first title, *The Heiress's 2-Week Affair*
by *USA TODAY* bestselling author
Marie Ferrarella, on sale in April!**

His 7-Day Fiancée by **Gail Barrett**	May
The 9-Month Bodyguard by **Cindy Dees**	June
Prince Charming for 1 Night by **Nina Bruhns**	July
Her 24-Hour Protector by **Loreth Anne White**	August
5 minutes to Marriage by **Carla Cassidy**	September

You're invited to join our Tell Harlequin Reader Panel!

By joining our new reader panel you will:

- Receive Harlequin® books—they are FREE and yours to keep with no obligation to purchase anything!
- Participate in fun online surveys
- Exchange opinions and ideas with women just like you
- Have a say in our new book ideas and help us publish the best in women's fiction

In addition, you will have a chance to win great prizes and receive special gifts!
See Web site for details. Some conditions apply.
Space is limited.

To join, visit us at

www.TellHarlequin.com.

Tell
HARLEQUIN

REQUEST YOUR FREE BOOKS!

2 FREE NOVELS PLUS 2 FREE GIFTS!

Silhouette® Romantic

SUSPENSE

Sparked by Danger, Fueled by Passion!